Acknowledgments and Thanks

I wish to thank the following people for their support and devotion as I wrote this novel. Their technical expertise ensured authenticity and greatly improved the final work.

- Lt. Colonel David Morris – Battle Creek Air National Guard (Retired)
- Captain Mark Sliwoski – USCG Licensed Master of Ocean-going Ships
- Phil Walsh – Islamic Cultural Consultant
- Ron Hoppock – F-18 Pilot, United States Navy (Retired)

The Saracen Tide

Skip
Coryell

Published by White Feather Press. (www.whitefeatherpress.com)

ISBN 978-1-61808-099-8

Printed in the United States of America

Cover design created by Ron Bell of AdVision Design Group
(www.advisiondesigngroup.com)

White Feather Press

Reaffirming Faith in God, Family, and Country!

Books by Skip Coryell

We Hold These Truths
Bond of Unseen Blood
Church and State
Blood in the Streets
Laughter and Tears
RKBA: Defending the Right to Keep and Bear Arms
Stalking Natalie
The God Virus
The Shadow Militia
The Saracen Tide

For Sara, my dear wife,
whom I love and fight for.

And to my Aunt Susie
who encourages me …
and kicks my butt
when I stop writing.

What has gone before...

In book one of this series, *The God Virus*, a cyber terrorist attack takes out the American power grid, leaving the entire country in darkness, death and widespread chaos. Dan Branch and his son, Jeremy, have to sojourn through Northern Wisconsin to the Michigan Lower Peninsula to the safety of his Uncle Rodney's home. Uncle Rodney, an eccentric, hardcore prepper and Vietnam vet tries to rescue Dan but fails.

It takes Dan and his son six months to reach the safety of the northern Lower Peninsula. On the way Dan is forced to kill many men. He also rescues Jackie, a damsel in distress, and marries her. When they finally reach Iroquois City, Uncle Rodney reveals he is the commanding general of *The Shadow Militia* and a mob of over a thousand cutthroats and thieves will be attacking within the week.

In book two, *The Shadow Militia*, Dan Branch, Uncle Rodney and Sheriff Leif lead the citizens of Iroquois county into battle against thousands of vicious and deadly gang members hell-bent on destroying anyone who resists their quest for power.

Through sheer tenacity and great sacrifice the army of cutthroats is stopped, but not before they destroy much of Iroquois City. Hundreds of townspeople are killed or wounded. The patriots of Iroquois county have earned a rest. But repose is not in the cards, because a new, larger and deadlier threat is on the way.

Will the Shadow Militia and the people of Iroquois be able to defeat this newest threat? The story begins where it left off. I am proud to give you ... *The Saracen Tide*!

PROLOGUE

Last Year - 48 Hours after "The Day"
Dearborn, Michigan

IMAM ABDUL AL'KALWI HAD CONSID-
ered killing his friend quietly, without the shame of
public humiliation, sparing him the suffering and pain
of watching his life's work slip away only inches from the
finish line. But, in the end, as much as he admired and loved
his closest friend, he realized that Allah craved the blood of
his mentor, and that he must die in a perfect and painless way.
After all, it was the least he could do for his friend. In a way,
he was doing him a favor. These were harsh and terrible times.
In his heart, Abdul knew that his friend, Mohammed, was just
not up to the challenge, even though his friend refused to see it
for what it was. Mohammed was weak; therefore, it was time
for his friend to enter into his paradise.

So he stood now beside Mohammed, their first in command, as he addressed the other Imams, laying out his plans
for the future. The electricity had been out all across America
for less than 48 hours, and already Mohammed was issuing
orders of moderation, of love and charity and mercy. They
were to reach out to the infidels, to offer them food and clothing and other forms of humanitarian aid, and in return the

Christians would treat the Muslim community with tolerance and kindness.

That was the plan, and it left a sour taste of bile in Abdul's mouth. His throat tightened as his friend continued speaking. They were in a lower room of the mosque, separated and private. Abdul would have preferred a more public execution, but that just wasn't possible. Nonetheless, it would do. So long as the Imams feared him they would follow him. The Imams would follow Abdul, and the people would follow the Imams. In that way, there would be order and no doubt about who was in control.

The scimitar was hidden beneath his robe, and his right hand tightened on the hilt of it now. Abdul was not like the other Imams. They were men of peace, soft men, well versed in the Koran, but not in the ways of war. In preparation for this day, Abdul had studied the history of war as well as the skills of battle. He was an excellent swordsman, physically strong and fit in the prime of his life. He and he alone was best suited to lead in time of war.

And the war was about to begin.

In one fluid, practiced motion, Abdul drew his sword as he stepped behind his leader. The sword came out and rose head high and plunged forward into the right side of his friend's neck. He felt resistance as the blade came against the vertebrae, but he pushed on through it in accordance with his studies, and his friend's head flopped down onto the floor with a thud. The rest of the body hung there for a second, like a suspended rag doll puppet, as blood spurted up from the headless neck, then it collapsed to the rug beside the head. Lifeless eyes looking up at Abdul, his friend, as if asking ... *why, why, why?*

In reply, Abdul nodded to his loyal conspirators and three more Imams were struck down in unison. Their cuts were not as precise as Abdul's, and he enjoyed his superiority for a moment. Then he made a mental note to make them practice their cuts.

2

In the space of twenty seconds all power had changed. The world was now on a different course. Imam Abdul Al'Kalwi smiled as the blood of his friend bumped up against his sandals and slowly soaked into the carpet.

CHAPTER 1

The Aftermath of War

DAN BRANCH SAT ON TOP OF THE Abrams tank looking down on the city. It had been three days since the end of battle, and he felt tired inside. There was an early spring rain filtering down now through a clouded sky, lending an eerie gloom to the town below. The tank's armor was wet and cold on his butt, and he shivered slightly as he watched the thin layer of snow melting on the ground all around him. It was a cleansing melt, and he welcomed it.

Most of the bodies were already buried, but it had been done in haste to prevent the spread of disease and to keep the smell down. In the mass graves they'd spread powdered lime on the bodies before covering them up to hasten the decomposition. With the rain and warmth of summer, the grass would grow and quickly wipe away most traces of death and battle. He glanced over at an oak tree just a few yards away. It was large, three feet in diameter, and had been burned and charred during his fire bomb attack on the very tank on which he was now perched. The tree would probably recover. Like the tree, Dan felt burned and charred, somehow fundamentally damaged inside. But ... he was alive, and so were his wife and children.

The town had been saved. But at what cost? Thousands of the enemy had been killed as well as hundreds of the townspeople, and, because of the nature of the battle, only a few prisoners had been taken. His Uncle Rodney had wanted to execute them on the spot, but Sheriff Leif had intervened and banished them from Iroquois county. It seemed like such a small matter, after so much other killing, but Dan had been glad to watch the dozen or so prisoners run off into the woods unharmed. It seemed symbolic and somehow important, like they had made a decision to hold on to at least a small shred of their humanity.

Dan used his gloved hands to pull the collar of his wool coat up around his neck. The chill was getting to him. He got up off the dead and blackened tank, jumped to the ground and headed home to his family.

And now, it was time to rebuild.

****

"But Uncle rodney, where are you going? We need you here!" Young Jeremy Branch stood in front of the door, blocking the path of his uncle who now stood poised to leave. The olive drab duffle bag was slung over his left shoulder, while his M4A1 carbine was clutched in his right hand. Uncle Rodney had become hard and tough over the last two months, but there was no longer a need for him here.

"I'm sorry, son. I'm needed elsewhere now."

Jackie stood off to one side looking on. She was smiling, not happy because he was leaving, rather privileged to have known him. She stepped forward now.

"Jeremy, it's okay. He'll be back if we're ever threatened. You can count on that."

Rodney looked into her eyes. They shared a moment of melding and trust. His eyes smiled and he found himself thinking. *She gets it. She really is a Branch.*

Jackie reached out and wrapped her arms around her uncle, pulling him close. He remained ramrod stiff for a moment, but then slowly softened his stance. The woman leaned in closer and put her mouth up to his ear before whispering softly.

"You made me a stronger person."

When Jackie pulled away she was smiling. Uncle Rodney's eyes moistened, but his face betrayed no hint of emotion.

"Make sure Daniel reads the letter."

General Branch pulled the M4 off his right shoulder and handed it to Jeremy. "Keep the family safe."

The young man reached out hesitantly before grasping it firmly in his hands. Without another word the general moved forward, skirting past his nephew and on out to the waiting helicopter. A few moments later it lifted off the ground and sped away into the rain-filled sky. Jackie and Jeremy watched from the porch until the tiny dot disappeared.

She went inside to tend to baby Donna, while Jeremy stood there in the drizzle, looking down at his new weapon. He moved his fingers over the collapsible stock and worked his way up to the rail system and barrel. It was getting wet, so he took one last look at the empty sky and then moved back inside to clean and oil his new carbine.

****

"He just left? He didn't even tell you good bye?" Sheriff Leif was looking down at the letter from General Branch. His fingers were trembling slightly. Dan Branch was sitting across from the Sheriff with his legs crossed one over the other, looking ahead blankly.

"I wasn't even there. He gave the letter to Jackie and then got in his chopper and flew away."

The sheriff lowered the letter and then looked up as he leaned back in his reclining office chair. "So when is he coming back?"

Dan folded his arms across his muscled torso. "Just read the letter. It says it all."

Joe Leif looked back down and read the letter aloud, pausing every so often to let it sink in.

> To: Sheriff Joe Leif and Colonel Dan Branch.
>
> From: Rodney Branch, Commanding General, Shadow Militia
>
> Subject: Change of Command

The sheriff stopped reading and looked over at Dan. "Looks like you've been promoted to colonel." Dan Branch didn't answer. He just looked off toward the window with an unseeing gaze.

> I, General Rodney Branch, do hereby relinquish command of all Iroquois county military forces to Colonel Daniel Branch. You have proven yourself in battle to be an honorable and formidable fighting commander. You are hereby charged with the defense of Iroquois county and the surrounding geography.

"The surrounding geography? What does that mean?"

Dan shrugged his shoulders and continued looking through the window. "I don't know. With Uncle Rodney that could mean the whole state of Michigan. Who knows?"

> You will continue to report to Sheriff Joe Leif, the only remaining constitution-ally elected civilian leader in your area. You will obey all orders given by him and support him as your resources allow, as I

have done in the past.

Sheriff Leif laughed out loud. "Obey me as he has done in the past? That old man never obeyed me a day in his life!"

Dan smiled for the first time that morning. "Yes, my uncle never did take orders very well."

The sheriff thought back to the interrogation of the captured horde sniper, how Rodney had feigned compliance, only to torture the man as soon as Joe left the jail cell. Rodney Branch subordinated himself to no man.

"True. But when he disobeyed me, he did it with such flair and personality that a part of me enjoyed it, almost couldn't wait to see what the old man would do next."

Dan nodded his head in agreement. "I love the man. But he scares the hell out of me."

The sheriff chuckled before reading on.

Your command priorities shall be as follows:

1. Continue to train, organize and enhance the military forces of Iroquois county.

2. Enter into a mutual defense alliance with neighboring counties and assist them in training and organization.

3. Support Sheriff Leif and other civilian units under his command in rebuilding the town.

"That sounds like a full time job to me. How are you going to do all that, Dan?"

Dan Branch uncrossed his legs and leaned forward in the chair. "Beats the hell outta me." Then he looked Joe square in the eyes. "So how are you going to rebuild the town, feed us, clothe us, and ward off disease?"

The sheriff broke the stare and looked over at the blank wall. "I have no idea. I don't feel any more capable now than I did before The Day."

Dan nodded his agreement. "Neither do I. But … I have a notion that our feelings don't really matter much anymore. It doesn't matter what we *feel* we can do; it matters what we actually *can* do." He looked out the window again. "And you have to admit, Joe, we have some accomplishments under our belts. We fought off thousands of deadly cutthroats and won. Yeah, sure, we had some help from Uncle Rodney and the Shadow Militia, but, in the end, what *we* did … *we* did."

The sheriff let that sink in for a moment or two. Then he looked away from the wall and met Dan's gaze again. "I suppose you're right. Almost everything we did over the past few months went against our feelings but we did them anyways. Just a few days ago I felt like giving up. I did, in fact, give up. But Rodney picked me up, dusted me off and put me back in command."

Dan smiled. "Yeah, I know what you mean. Even when I was a kid, my uncle had this way of helping me believe I could do things I wasn't capable of. He always pushed me to my limit and then another ten percent."

Sheriff Leif looked back down at the letter and soberly read the valediction.

> I write these instructions in my own hand, and they are to be carried out until further orders. It is with a heavy heart that I leave you to your own defense. But know this: if I can assist you in the future, I will. You are more than friends and conquerors. You have come through the fire, and you are as shining brass. You will do more than survive. With God's grace and strength, you will prevail and you will flourish.

Your brother in arms,

General Rodney T. Branch

Commanding General
The Shadow Militia

Sheriff Leif tossed the letter on his desk and shook his head from side to side. "Your uncle is the weirdest person I've ever known."

Dan Branch nodded his head and smiled. "You got that right." He hesitated a moment. "So what are we going to do?"

The sheriff swiveled nervously back and forth a few seconds in his office chair. Finally, he answered. "That old man knows more than he's saying. And it grinds me to admit that he's always been right in the past. The only sensible thing to do is follow his advice and just wait until whatever he knows is gonna happen, happens. At least then we'll be ready for it, or, as ready as we can be."

Dan Branch stood to his feet moved his palms over his shirt to straighten out the wrinkles. "I got some thinking to do and people to talk to. Shall we meet here tomorrow morning at zero eight hundred hours?"

Sheriff Leif laughed out loud, cognizant that Uncle Rodney lived on in his nephew. "Sure thing, Colonel. Eight o'clock sounds good to me. You bring the donuts."

CHAPTER 2

Major Danskill

T WAS EARLY SPRING IN NORTHERN Michigan, and a tiny wisp of smoke curled up out of the wooded ravine. The rain had stopped, leaving Major Danskill soaking wet and shivering in his olive drab field jacket. His hands shook as he pulled the collar up over his bare neck. The major leaned forward and stirred the red coals of the fire with a stick, then he tossed the limb onto the coals and watched as the heat blackened the wood before bursting it into flames.

He mumbled to himself, "Know your enemy." He hated Sun Tzu more than ever now. Why hadn't he taken his time, gathered more intel? Instead, he'd blundered into a trap set by the leader of the Shadow Militia. He thought about General Rodney Branch, his adversary, his enemy, and then he thought of the Blind Man. They were two sides to the same coin. Both were powerful, determined and cunning, and Danskill knew in his heart that planet Earth wasn't big enough for the both of them. One of them had to die. But which one? That was the question. And which one was most likely to let him live? On the one hand he hated General Branch, because he'd been humiliated and defeated by him on the field of battle. Danskill had held all the cards, but Branch had bested him regardless. On the other hand, the Blind Man had the power to pick up the phone and have him eliminated. Or, he could capture him for interrogation. The major thought that was probably the most likely option of the two. The Blind Man would be desperate for intel. Like Sun Tzu he'd want to know his enemy. Danskill had information the Blind Man needed to know, and that could be the key to not only keeping him alive, but also to returning him to power.

They would be picking him up soon. In the quiet of the woods, Major Danskill made his decision. His best chance for glory was with the Blind Man. And then … there was always the matter of his unnatural appetites. The Blind Man would feed them so long as Danskill was a tool of value. But, in his heart, he knew that General Branch, a man of honor, could not and would not condone such practices.

COLONEL MACPHERSON LOWERED THE BINOCULARS from his eyes and thought for a moment. "What's he doing down there, Donny?"

Sergeant Brewster shook his head back and forth. "I don't know, Colonel. He appears to be hugging himself and rocking back and forth."

Mac closed his eyes and listened, but no sounds save the wind in the trees came to him. "He's waiting, sergeant. They're coming for him." He looked down at the man beside the campfire, expecting the sound of an extraction helicopter at any moment. "We need to hurry. Get set up and take the shot."

Iroquois City HQ - 8AM

"SO WHAT IS YOUR FIRST MOVE, DAN?" SHERIFF LEIF looked across the conference room table at his military counterpart. Colonel Dan Branch, now dressed in pressed and starched military fatigues, stood up and walked over to the white board. The county courthouse had been cleared of rubble, and repairs were already underway. Structurally it was still sound.

"I've already assigned Major Jackson with the formidable task of reorganizing what's left of the Home Guard and the Militia Rangers. Captain Alvarez is in charge of logistics. He'll be collecting every weapon and ordinance he can find as well as developing new weapons systems. Captain Brown will head up training."

Dan wrote in block letters on the white board.

MAJOR JACKSON - REORGANIZATION

CAPTAIN ALVAREZ - LOGISTICS

CAPTAIN BROWN - TRAINING

"So what are *you* going to do, Dan?" Colonel Branch didn't say anything, he simply wrote on the white board in response to the sheriff's question.

COLONEL BRANCH - DEFENSE ALLIANCES

Sheriff Joe Leif nodded his head and folded his arms across his chest. "That means you'll have to travel." He hesitated. "Does Jackie know?"

Dan caught his drift and smiled to himself. It was no secret to the inner circle that his wife was very protective of him and hadn't appreciated his absence in the last battle. Even though she understood the extreme circumstances, a woman just didn't appreciate being away from her man. After all, technically, they were still newlyweds.

"No, not yet." He looked over at the sheriff, the only other man in the room. "Any ideas?"

Sheriff Leif thought for a moment. "She needs to feel important, and she's a very capable woman. I could use her in helping to rebuild the town. That wouldn't make her feel happy about you leaving, but it would give her something to do. And I need all the help I can get."

Dan nodded appreciatively. "Thanks Joe." He stepped away from the white board and back to his seat. "So what about you? What plans do you have?"

Joe Leif answered his question by sliding a sheet of yellow ruled paper across the table to him. Dan read the hand-scribbled notes silently.

Priorities

1. Food - gather food, plant crops, set up distribution system.

2. Organize medical personnel & supplies and schedule physical exam for all citizens.

3. Rebuild as time and supplies allow.

4. Set up system to handle refugees. Who goes - who stays.

5. Establish laws for births, marriages, deaths, transfer of property and commerce.

"I don't envy you, Sheriff."

Joe scoffed. "Hell, my job is easy compared to what you're going to be doing. I can't even imagine how you're going to convince people from other counties to train, prepare and equip for war when all they're worried about is feeding their families."

The sheriff paused and waited for an answer, but none came. He pushed it a bit further. "So, Dan, exactly how are you going to do it?"

Colonel Branch hesitated and gazed out the window at the brown grass on the courthouse lawn. It would be turning green soon. Finally, he answered.

"I'm going to offer them hope."

Sheriff Leif smiled. "And if that doesn't work?"

Dan laughed out loud. "Well … then I'll have to just scare the hell out of 'em. I'll figure something out."

Joe smiled softly and looked down at the table in front of them. "Any word from your uncle yet?"

That was the unspoken question, the one all the townspeople had been asking. "Where is General Rodney T. Branch?" Dan thought it ironic that all his life the people of Iroquois had tolerated his uncle, viewed him as an oddity, wondered in hush tones about his very sanity. And now, they held him up as their hope, as their hero, as their savior. But what happens when your hero is gone? Who do you believe in then?

Somehow, Dan and Joe had to inspire them, give them hope, and a reason to fight and rebuild. Both men stood up and left the room, hurrying about to their appointed impossible tasks.

CHAPTER 3

Dearborn, Michigan

ON THE DAY THE LIGHTS WENT OUT, the city of Dearborn, Michigan held the largest population of Muslims in the United States and the second densest Muslim population outside the Middle East, second only to Paris, France. Within days Sharia law had been firmly imposed in the city, and had already begun to spread to the outlying areas as the Muslim population branched out. As the events of The Day unfolded and Abdul Al'Kalwi quickly established unchallenged control of the region, he gave himself a new title, Supreme General Abdul Al'Kalwi. This coincided with his plan of conquest and eradication of all infidels first in Michigan and then the entire Midwest.

Within several months after The Day, Abdul had put to death all Jews and Christians refusing to convert to Islam. Thousands were publicly executed, as the streets ran red with kafir blood. The only infidels to survive were those who had recognized the threat early on and fled to the outlying rural areas. The Supreme General's plan was simple. Move west across the state like a Saracen tide, cleansing the land of all non-Islamic influence. In accordance with the Koran, the Hadith, and the Sura all kafirs who refused to convert would be put to death with the sword.

Now that thousands had already been beheaded, the other infidels would swear allegiance to Allah and to the Supreme

General.

But before he could advance, he first needed to control two things: military hardware and the local food source. To do this he immediately seized control of all the local armories and food warehouses. Under normal circumstances this would have been difficult to near impossible, but after The Day most of the armories were lightly guarded and disorganized. Many military personnel had gone home to protect their families and would not be back. A few of the small arms had been pilfered, but Abdul found most weapons intact. He started out by taking the smallest armory first; that gave him the weapons he needed to move on to larger prey. Within a week's time, the Supreme General had gained control of hundreds of military trucks of all shapes and sizes: Humvees, light and medium military tactical vehicles, even some Heavy Expanded Mobility Tactical Trucks which were eight-wheel drive diesel-powered off-road capable vehicles. By the time he reached Selfridge Air National Guard base in Mt. Clemons just north of Detroit, Abdul felt unstoppable.

But what he found there was nothing but empty aircraft hangers and tarmac. The F-16 Fighter jets and the A10 Warthog ground support aircraft were nowhere to be seen.

In a fit of rage, Abdul had drawn his broadsword and decapitated the man closest to him. From his study of military history, he knew that airpower would make him invincible, especially in a world without electricity thrown back into the middle ages. But now, without military air support, his own vast army would be vulnerable from the air.

Despite the setback, Abdul had spent the first winter after The Day consolidating his hold on eastern Michigan all the way up to the thumb area. Where chaos once reigned, the Supreme General offered the people a system of order, food and purpose. Every day people lined up at designated distribution centers for their daily allotment of food. They never received more than one day's rations, which ensured they would always be forced to depend solely on him for the bread of life. In return, all he asked was submission to Allah and to himself. It was a fair trade … submission for life.

All through the winter months Abdul had organized and planned his spring offensive. By April the weather had cleared and he'd amassed twenty thousand troops: half conscripts and the other half loyal Muslims of Middle Eastern descent.

Finally, on a sunny day in mid-April, he stood at the top of one of the minarets at the Islamic Center of America looking out across the vast encampment. He liked coming up here to look at his army. It was huge and extended out as far as he could see. And he controlled it all. Abdul watched as the hundreds of trucks were loaded with supplies for their push west. They would move slowly, scavenging and raping the land as they went. There was no hurry. They would move straight down the US Highway 94 corridor all the way to Jackson. From there he'd divide his forces, half going north to Lansing to secure the capitol and the other half continuing on west to Kalamazoo.

Once both major cities were pacified, the two armies would move toward Grand Rapids in a double-pronged attack. He expected to subdue all of southwest Michigan in a few months. Then he would move south to northern Indiana and then west to winter in Chicago. Wherever they went, his plan was to clear a swath twenty miles on either side of his advancing army, gathering supplies, recruiting soldiers, and slaughtering all who resisted Islam.

The Supreme General looked out over his army and then up into the lightly clouded sky. It was a good day to follow the prophet.

The Blind Man

JARED THOMPSON SAT ALONE AT THE CONFERENCE TABLE in his own, private situation room. When he was alone he didn't have to feign blindness, and that freed him up to get more work done. He read over the reports from the various regional commanders. They had pacified most of the cities on the west and east coasts. In fact, the eastern and western seaboards were his firmest strongholds. But the center of the country continued to elude him. The Rocky mountains were rife with rebels, while the Appalachians were still saturated with rednecks on the rise. It seemed like every rock had a freedom fighter hiding underneath it. *Why did they hang on to their liberty with such vehemence?* In his heart of hearts, Jared knew most of them would have to be killed. He threw up his hands and smiled. "Oh well. You can't make an omelet without breaking a few eggs."

Then he looked up at the large video screen on the wall. He pressed a few buttons, zooming in on Michigan. Here, he hadn't expected such resistance, such a concentration of unforeseen power. He needed more intel, and that's why he'd dispatched his right-hand man, Sammy Thurmond, to bring in Major Danskill. The National Guard commander would tell him everything he wanted to know, one way or another.

Escanaba, Michigan

GENERAL RODNEY BRANCH HAD JUST RETURNED FROM Montana, and every muscle of his tired old body was sore and felt like giving up. For the past two weeks he'd been in nonstop travel mode, reviewing troops in Kentucky, advising resistance in Kansas, and meeting with rebels in Texas. Now, he sat on the edge of the cot in Colonel MacPherson's lavish mansion in the Upper Peninsula. Rodney had been overjoyed to learn that his best friend, Colonel Roger "Ranger" MacPherson had survived the battle for Iroquois County.

Rodney smiled when he recalled their first meeting decades ago in Vietnam. They'd both been young officers, just starting out on their journey to become master warriors. They had bonded the next few years, fighting a war neither understood nor enjoyed. Both men had learned much from the Vietcong, and Rodney suspected he'd need all his skill and cunning to defeat the enemy now trying to enslave America.

Mac had never understood why his commanding general always insisted on such common quarters. In fact, the room Rodney now slept in was nothing more than a walk-in closet with a cot, foot locker, nightstand and metal wall locker. Mac and Rodney had grown up in opposite worlds. Mac was the man of privilege, growing up with a silver spoon in his mouth, but on reaching adulthood, he'd rejected the plush lifestyle in favor of the ascetic warrior life. On his father's death, Mac had inherited a fortune composed mainly of research and development facilities and defense manufacturing plants scattered across the country. This had given the Shadow Militia their teeth in the form of all the arms and supplies they could ever use.

Mac and Rodney were the two founding members of the Shadow Militia, and over the course of thirty plus years they'd built the organization one recruit at a time. Mac, who had retired from the military after thirty years at the rank of Major General had hand-picked all the Shadow Militia personnel. Rodney had spent several years in the Marine Corps before transferring to the Army. When his brother died, he'd been forced to retire early to raise his nephew. Rodney had remained the strategic planner, because he could do that from the obscurity of Iroquois county. Mac, despite his superior rank and experience, had insisted Rodney command the group. They had turned out to be the perfect team to fight the second war for independence.

Just then, there was a knock on the closet door. Out of habit, Rodney placed his right hand on the 1911 pistol on his right hip. "Enter!" He relaxed when the door opened and Sergeant Donny Brewster walked in and stood at attention.

"The Colonel is waiting, sir."

General Branch smiled and nodded to the seasoned, young sniper. "Very well, Sergeant. Please inform the Colonel I'll be down in fifteen minutes." Rodney pulled on his olive drab fatigues and began buttoning up his shirt. He was surprised to see Donny still standing there.

"What's up, Sergeant?"

Donny hesitated before answering.

"Permission to speak candidly about a personal matter, sir?"

The General smiled for the first time since returning to Michigan. "Permission granted." He finished buttoning his shirt and moved to pulling on his pants.

"Sir, I would like to be temporarily assigned to Iroquois County."

Rodney thought for a moment. "And why is your duty station considered personal?"

The sergeant squirmed a bit, and Rodney found it amusing. Here was a highly trained, dedicated warrior with hundreds of kills to his credit, and he was nervous over a simple administrative request. It didn't make any sense. And then a light went on in the general's head.

"Ahh, I see now." Rodney laughed out loud. "This wouldn't happen to have anything to do with a certain young nurse, a very pretty and confident nurse?"

The young sniper lowered his head slightly and came close to blushing.

"Is it that obvious, sir?"

Rodney was standing now, buttoning his freshly starched olive-drab trousers. He took a half-step forward.

"At ease, Sergeant."

Donny's left foot stepped to the side and his hands moved behind his back. The grizzly old general looked his young charge directly in the eye.

"So, as long as we're speaking candidly, is it lust or love?"

A slight smile tweaked the corner of Donny's mouth. "Well, sir. I have vast experience with lust, but when it comes to love, I fear I'm just a lowly private." He hesitated as if forming his next words carefully. "However, in this case, I think it might be both, sir."

The General nodded. "I see. Well, you sure picked a hell of a time to fall in love, Sergeant."

Donny didn't know how to respond. "Yes sir. I understand, sir."

Rodney sat back down on the cot and pulled on first one black boot and then the other. He laced them up as Donny waited in suspense. The General seemed to enjoy his nervousness. When he was done, Rodney stood to his full height with a grim face.

"So what was her name again?"

"Lisa, sir."

General Branch nodded.

"And what color are her eyes?"

"Blue, sir. Aqua blue. Like Lake Michigan in mid-summer when it's really warm, and the sun is shining, and the birds are singing ..."

"Okay, okay! That's enough! I get the picture!" The General thought for a moment as if going over a million details in his mind. "Let me double-check with Mac, first. But I think we can swing some temporary duty to northern Lower Michigan. While you're down there you can assist Colonel Branch in training and reorganizing his forces. Understood?"

Sergeant Brewster snapped rigidly to attention.

"Sir, yes sir!"

Rodney turned away.

"Good, now let's go down and see what the Colonel has for us on this Major Danskill situation."

Rodney abruptly left the room, followed by Donny Brewster. General Branch paused long enough to place the padlock back on the door before striding briskly away with Donny in tow.

CHAPTER 4

Life in Iroquois County

AFTER THE BATTLE OF **I**ROQUOIS County people tried to get back to the business of not only surviving, but also of improving their way of life. Because of the cosmos and stability put in place by Sheriff Leif, and defended by Colonel Branch, reconstruction work began on the city. It was slow going, because the daily lives of most people were occupied in growing and gathering food, bringing in firewood for the next winter, and in general, healing both physically and emotionally from the scars of war and the harshness of colonial-era life.

Sheriff Leif held a county-wide meeting in order to disseminate new laws and to gain consensus on a provision-sharing program. Joe felt uncomfortable with this, because to some it seemed like a forced tax. In the end the people agreed to give ten percent of their goods or labor to a county-wide reserve to be used during time of emergency. This was only possible due to the popularity and trust accrued by Sheriff Leif over a period of twenty years of living a life of integrity with the citizens of Iroquois.

Despite that, a small minority resisted and refused to sign on. Joe tried to bring them into the cooperative, but in the end, they'd refused. Joe publicly acknowledged their ability to choose their own destiny, which seemed to boost his popularity even higher. He confided with Dan that he just couldn't bring himself to force compliance on his friends and neighbors. The people of Northern Michigan had always been a tough and independent breed, and this had become even more the case after The Day.

The citizens rebuilt the churches and the school first, and by June they held a grand re-opening ceremony and feast. Pot-luck dinners used to be commonplace in frontier America, but had faded into disuse with the advent of modern entertainment, computers, sports bars and TV dinners. Now that electricity was all but extinct, the pot-luck dinner once again flourished. And although life was hard, there were unforeseen benefits. Prior to The Day, Iroquois suffered from a fifty percent divorce rate. In post-apocalypse Iroquois, that percentage dropped to almost zero. In fact, the only divorce request came from an older couple whom Joe had known his entire life. He tried to talk them out of it, but they'd insisted. Joe drew up divorce papers for them which they promptly signed. Then, to the Sheriff's chagrin, the old man and woman had kissed and went on home to live their lives as usual.

Drug and alcohol abuse had been prevalent in all of Northern Michigan, but since drugs and alcohol were in very short supply, those addicted quickly became unaddicted. One less thing.

After the Battle of Iroquois County crime dropped to almost nothing, and those crimes that were committed originated from outside the county, usually by drifters.

In accordance with his orders from General Branch, Dan worked with Joe to hunt down the criminals, which sometimes meant entering other counties to bring them to justice. Several times posses were formed just like in the Old West, thus, in doing so, the citizens were given an active hand in enforcing the laws they lived by. The laws and punishments were harsh but fair and necessary. After a fair and speedy trial, most evil-doers were given a brand on their right forearm of the letter "C", which meant criminal. They were then banished from Iroquois, and their return would result in immediate execution.

In post-apocalypse Iroquois, there was no such thing as rehabilitation. They didn't have the logistics to handle prisoners for more than a few weeks at a time. Serious crimes like attempted rape, rape, child molestation, attempted murder, murder and kidnapping held the death sentence and were carried out within twenty-four hours after trial with a single bullet to the head. But as of June only two executions had taken place, and those were former convicts from Jackson Prison who had wandered into the area. Sheriff Leif carried out the sentence personally in front of the courthouse for all citizens to see.

Before The Day Iroquois county had boasted a population of fifty-three thousand people. Almost all the casualties of war had been replaced, and now, they held steady at close to fifty thousand men, women and children. Throughout northern Michigan, Iroquois had gained the reputation of being a calm amidst the storm, a place to raise your family with the possibility of passing on that lifestyle to your children. Sheriff Leif had a backlog of residency applications, so he appointed a committee to winnow out the undesirables, thus making his job less time consuming. Of course certain people were highly sought after such as medical personnel, civil engineers, and Mennonites as well as Amish families, because of their extensive experience in frontier living. Almost on a daily basis either Colonel Branch or one of the other county leaders would come to Joe with a request for a certain skill. If that skill couldn't be met inside the county, then an applicant was offered Iroquois county citizenship. The offer was always accepted.

Colonel Branch used Militia forces to set up a series of listening posts all around the county border. All major roads were manned and guarded complete with radio communication. There was no longer any shortage of military manpower as most residents were now seasoned combat veterans.

Anyone with sickness was not allowed to pass through as tens of thousands had died downstate from disease and malnutrition.

But the flood of refugees had slowed to a trickle by summer's start as most people hadn't prepared and had simply died of cold, starvation, disease or lawlessness during the first winter. So, because of their newfound reputation of fairness, strength and mild living conditions, Iroquois continued to grow and prosper while others suffered.

Indeed, several of the contiguous counties were in dire straits, so Colonel Branch traveled there first to offer them aid in return for joining a mutual defense pact with the strongest county of the region. Initially, Dan thought his job would be near to impossible, but he'd underestimated the power of legend and reputation. To those outside of Iroquois, the stories had spread of grand and glorious battle, how the Home Guard and Militia Rangers had stood up to a mighty horde of a million men and won using sheer courage and determination. Dan allowed them to believe what they wished, since it made his job so much easier.

And then ... there were always the stories of the ever elusive and powerful ... the Shadow Militia.

Dan made good use of Sergeant Donny Brewster in training the Home Guard and Military Rangers. The Guard received basic combat instruction, whereas the Rangers began intensive Special Forces training. They may never rival SEALS, but neither would they ever be mere farmers again.

Anyone with exceptional aptitude and ability in marksmanship was put into a special unit to undergo sniper training. Donny trained them personally, and, despite Dan's protests, Jeremy Branch had been one of his first recruits. Jeremy was now sixteen years old and a crack shot with any type of firearm. He had the gift.

But perhaps the biggest surprise of all was the contribution of Jackie Branch. She was appointed second in command of civilian forces by Sheriff Leif and served as a sworn Special Deputy, reporting directly to Joe. Her first project was to organize all the women of the county into a force capable of feeding and caring for its inhabitants. But to do that, first she had to educate them. Jackie formed a hard-working team (assisted by Marge Leif) and they began by interviewing every woman in the county, cataloging her strengths, weaknesses, her skills, and what training was necessary to better serve her own family as well as the community.

Every night a different community education class was held at the courthouse on such topics as home canning, food dehydration, family medicine, gardening, how to identify wild herbs, mushrooms and grasses, cooking with wood, doing laundry by hand and home sanitation methods. To accomplish this she drew on many older members of the county who had lived through the Great Depression and the Second World War. She also raided the local museums and auction houses for antiques which were promptly taken out of mothballs and put into service. Due to the hard work and innovative thinking of Jackie Branch, the abrupt move from computer age to frontier-era life became a much smoother transition.

Because of the harshness of life, people pulled together, not because they were superior in any way, but simply out of necessity and leadership by example.

CHAPTER 5

General Branch and the Big Decision

RODNEY BRANCH SAT AT THE CON-
ference table beside his lifelong friend, Colonel
Roger "Ranger" MacPherson. He squinted his
eyes and furled his brow as he pondered the question before
him: a question, whose answer could either save or doom the
race of men in North America.

"I want your opinion, Mac. What do you think? Is this reli-
able?" He paused. "Or is this just wishful thinking of an old
man and too good to be true?"

The colonel met his gaze head on. He knew what the general was thinking. *If I make the wrong decision, thousands
will die, and it will be on my head.* Mac smiled inside. He
had been here many times himself while still a general in the
Army Rangers, and he didn't envy his friend one bit. Several
times Mac had made the "wrong decision" and innocent and
brave soldiers had died unnecessarily. It was inevitable. No
one could be right all the time. The difference was when a
sergeant made a bad call, perhaps ten men could die. When a
general screwed up it could mean the lives of thousands.

But none of that mattered right now. Mac knew it and so
did Rodney. But Colonel MacPherson took it by the numbers
and slowly mapped it out for his friend.

"It's the best intelligence we have, General. We don't have
eyes on The Blind Man, but the technology is sound and reli-

able. Right now, even as we speak, we believe The Blind Man to be interrogating Major Danskill deep inside a rock fortress in the mountains of Pennsylvania."

General Branch was deep in thought. He knew that Mac was simply stating the obvious, leading him to a decision pre-ordained by the facts and the desperate situation.

"We don't have a choice, do we Mac?"

The colonel didn't answer. He knew it wasn't really a question, just part of the decision-making process. The general would have to think it out, talk it out, and then go with his gut. That was Rodney's best trait as a commanding general. He had instincts that Mac did not.

"I understand that most commanders would jump at this chance but … it just seems too easy to me. Something doesn't feel right, Mac. Something is giving me pause. On the one hand, we could move in with bunker busters and level the place. We could bury the guy beneath his own rubble, but then we'd never find him, wouldn't even know if he was dead or alive. And if we failed … if the guy got away, then he would never underestimate us again. He would realize the Shadow Militia is the most real threat he faces. And isn't that why we refused to employ our forces in defense of Iroquois?"

Mac didn't answer. He simply waited for the general to talk himself out. General Branch looked over at his friend for help, knowing in advance that none would be there save the moral support and undying devotion of the strongest of men who would carry out his orders or die trying. General Branch sighed wearily and came to a decision.

"I want eyes-on surveillance from all four compass points over the next three days before we act. I want to know even the most mundane details of what goes on there. We can't underestimate The Blind Man. After that I want you to put together two plans: the first, an air strike using bunker busters, and the second, a conventional ground attack without air support. When it's all assembled and ready to launch, we'll talk again."

Colonel MacPherson stood up and swiftly strode out of the room. He was at his best when planning a mission. The only thing he enjoyed more than planning was leading the attack. Despite that, his general's orders confused him. *A ground attack without air support?* That was dangerous, risky and against all logic. But he didn't say anything, and he would carry out Rodney's orders to the letter. He had chosen his general, and everything in their life-long experience had taught him to trust Rodney's judgment and his instincts. He wouldn't change that now.

The Blind Man and Major Danskill

JARED THOMPSON WORE A TAILORED BLUE SUIT, SHINY, black Armani shoes and dark sunglasses. He liked to cover his eyes during interrogations; it freed him up to look directly into his victim's eyes without their knowledge. He called them victims, simply because he seldom interrogated anyone and left them alive. On many occasions the illusion of his blindness had given him an edge, because people were more free with their facial expressions when they believed they were being interrogated by someone who couldn't see them.

"So, Major Danskill, that's a very interesting story." He hesitated for a moment to build the suspense. "But it fails to impress me. I elevated you to a position of power. I gave you all the right military toys to play with." He hesitated. "I even suffered and fed your somewhat unusual tastes in young boys, which, of course. I deplore, being a man of moral integrity myself." He paused before going on. "But, to each his own I suppose. Far be it from me to judge."

Major Danskill was duct-taped naked to the wooden chair. The rest of the room was empty, sterile and bright white. It had been scrubbed and bleached to a cleanliness that would make a hospital operating room blush.

"In short, Major Danskill, why did you fail me?"

31

The major raised his chin up off his chest and looked directly into The Blind Man's eyes before speaking.

"I failed because of my own arrogance. Arrogance is a weakness that was exploited by our enemy. I thought I was fighting an organized band of farmers, when in fact, they were trained and led by General Rodney T. Branch, commanding general of The Shadow Militia."

Jared Thompson's heart quickened. He already knew this, but there was something about the spoken word that gave the fact more power. On the one hand, he relished and welcomed the challenge of a worthy adversary; on the other, he was determined to move ahead flawlessly and without impulse. He had to be right. He had to move slowly.

"Tell me all you know about General Rodney T. Branch."

Major Danskill knew this was his one chance to make himself useful, and if he failed, well, he knew The Blind Man wasn't the sort of person to collect useless baggage. The problem was he knew very little of General Branch or The Shadow Militia. So, because he would be killed if The Blind Man had no use for him, then he had no other choice, but to lie.

"To meet a man on the field of combat is to learn of him in the most intimate of details. I didn't know him beforehand or I would have won the battle. But, with each defeat comes knowledge and power. I learned about my adversary as I grappled with him. Then, afterwards, I became a spy in the camp of my enemy and I …"

But Jared Thompson was no longer listening to the man's fabrications. He'd already studied carefully the full biography of Rodney Branch. The general had an above-average IQ, but was by no means a genius. He had a college degree, but had graduated in the middle of his class. In fact, the only place Rodney Branch had ever excelled was on the field of battle. Somehow, some way, Rodney Branch always came out on top. He had a history of being put into hopeless situations and still winning. He was unpredictable, creative and he possessed courage, integrity and unequaled tenacity. And it was that last trait which impressed Jared the most. Sure, the courage and creativity made Rodney dangerous to him, and he would have recruited the general for his own purposes had he not possessed the flaw of integrity. But it was the tenacity that made him so deadly. Deep in his gut, Jared knew that tenacity never gave up; it just came after you over and over again until you killed it or it killed you.

Looking at Major Danskill ramble on about his qualities while he sat naked, duct-taped to a chair caused him to smile inside. This man would be of no use to him. He motioned for Sammy Thurmond, who had been at his right hand the entire time.

Sammy moved forward and pulled out a knife. Major Danskill stopped talking. The blade flicked open and cut the duct tape binding the major's hands. Danskill flexed his wrists to get the blood flowing again, and then he looked up and straight into The Blind Man's eyes.

Jared was seldom disconcerted, but this act more than anything else was uncomfortable to him. Somehow this man knew or sensed his sight. Jared wanted to know why, but his curiosity wasn't strong enough to spare the major's life.

Sammy Thurmond backed away, putting the knife into his pocket. Danskill couldn't stand as other tape still firmly affixed his butt to the chair. He could move his hands, but he wasn't going anywhere.

Jared Thompson then got up from his own chair and took a few steps forward. He took off his sunglasses and returned the major's gaze.

"How did you know?"

The major smiled. "Suffice it to say … I knew."

Jared nodded and pulled the small caliber handgun out of his suit pocket.

"There's only one bullet. I'd like you to shoot yourself. I recommend a shot to the head to minimize your suffering.

After all, you have been a faithful servant. However, you understand. I cannot allow you to live. It's nothing personal. You've always been very polite and congenial."

The major nodded once, his smile dissolving like late morning mist. He thought to himself, *I'm a warrior, and I won't go down without a fight. The Blind Man has to know this. He would never hand me a loaded gun.* Danskill reached out and accepted the pistol; it appeared to be a 32 caliber semiautomatic. Once he grasped the gun in his hands, he felt a wave of hope wash over him. *One bullet ... just one bullet. You'd best use it wisely.* A plan was already forming in his mind.

He moved the gun to his right hand and slowly slid back the slide just far enough to confirm a round was in the chamber. His heart skipped a beat when he saw the tail end of the shining brass. *One round, he had one round!*

Without hesitation he pulled the pistol up and placed the front sight between Sammy Thurmond's eyes. He quickly pulled the trigger.

Silence.

He pulled the trigger again. Nothing.

The major's heart sank, knowing he would soon be dead.

"Interesting. Very interesting. You had only one bullet, so you decided to kill the greatest threat first. Then you would no doubt have crushed the chair beneath you and killed me with your bare hands." Jared smiled. "I know all about you as well, Major Danskill. You are an expert in several martial art forms, are you not?"

Sammy Thurmond moved forward and took the pistol from Danskill's hand. There was no resistance. Then he stepped back and handed it to his boss. Jared hefted the gun back and forth in his hands, then he reached into his left coat pocket and took out a ring. He placed the ring on his right ring finger, and then pulled the gun up, pointing it directly at Major Danskill's head.

"You see, Major Danskill, this is a smart gun, and the ring sends out a signal to the chip in the pistol, thereby unlocking the firing mechanism. As long as I'm wearing the ring, and the gun is in my hand, the gun will fire, but minus the ring, this gun is simply a very expensive club, and a small club at that."

For a brief moment, Danskill thought of all the glory owed him that would never be paid. He thought of all the young boys he'd abused, and the ones who had gotten away.

Jared Thompson pressed the trigger, slowly and steadily to the rear. The shot rang out, and Major Danskill's head jerked back and then slumped forward onto his chest.

The Blind Man nonchalantly handed the gun over to Sammy Thurmond, who immediately put it into his pocket.

"Mr. Thurmond, after the autopsy, I would like you to take this body and cut it in half. Half the body will receive a proper funeral with full military honors. The other half will be taken to the woods nearby and tied to a tree, where wild animals will rip it to shreds and devour it."

He turned and looked into Sammy's eyes. He rarely did that. "Do you understand, Mr. Thurmond?"

Sammy quickly nodded. "Yes sir. It will be done as you command."

The Blind Man replaced his sunglasses, and put his left hand on Sammy's arm to be led from the room.

CHAPTER 6

Donny Brewster's Last Night Alive

"Yes, I'm afraid it's true. I ship out in the morning on a very dangerous mission. I'll likely not survive. This will undoubtedly be the last time you see me."

Lisa Vanderboeg raised her left eyebrow, and the hint of a smile touched her lips. "Really? You must be terrified."

Donny Brewster shrugged his muscular shoulders nonchalantly. "No, not really. Us soldiers face death every day. We stare it in the eyes and we mock its existence." He looked out past her into the playground, feigning contemplation. "Yes, to a warrior, death is more of a release than a punishment."

Lisa's blonde hair had grown longer since her first meeting with General Branch, so she grabbed a lock of curls and flipped it back behind her. She spoke her mind as always.

"What a screwed-up world view you have, Donny. That is, if you really believe this cock-and-bull story you're feeding me."

She looked at him with more than a small measure of skepticism. Donny's gaze moved back to her face, then a hurt look came over him, which Lisa didn't know was real or contrived.

"What? You don't believe me?"

"Of course I believe you. I believe that you're shipping out in the morning and that it's probably a dangerous mission, but I don't for a moment believe you're terrified. On the contrary,

I think you're excited about it; that you can't wait to get there and feel that adrenaline. I think you like killing people."

Something in Donny Brewster magically changed, and, this time, Lisa knew it was real. His face clouded over as his eyes moved off into the distance again.

"Is that why you don't like me, Lisa? Because I kill people?"

The young, blonde nurse squirmed on the park bench as her 5-year-old daughter played on the monkey bars with three other children her age.

"I didn't say I don't like you, Donny."

"But you didn't say you did either."

"It's complicated."

"How so?"

She looked off into the distance, trying to form her thoughts in a way that wouldn't hurt him any more than necessary.

"I'm not judging you. I've killed people too you know."

Donny turned back to her. "And what did it feel like for you?"

She shrugged her shoulders, not believing she was having this conversation. "Well, the first time my husband was in danger and I was in a fit of rage and terror. I didn't feel guilt. I just felt it was something that had to be done to protect the ones I love."

Donny turned back to face her. He looked into her deep, blue eyes.

"And the second time?"

"The second time I was with you at The Horde encampment. I was shooting a machine gun into the darkness. It wasn't so personal, and I just felt afraid and confused."

"Did you feel like you were doing the right thing?"

She thought about it a moment before answering.

"I suppose so. I mean The Horde was coming after us and would have killed my daughter if they'd made it here."

She made eye contact with Donny again.

"But it's different for you, because you enjoy it."

"And that's what you don't like about me?"

She nodded, almost ashamed of herself as she did so.

"I think so, yes. But the odd thing is, despite that, I still want you to exist. I want you to be there doing what you do best. I just don't want to be around it. I don't want to become like you. I don't want my little girl to grow up alongside a killer."

Donny flinched when he heard her say that as if she'd stabbed him with a knife. Then he looked out at little Samantha playing. All of a sudden he didn't want to be around Lisa anymore.

"I *am* a killer, Lisa. I was born and bred for it. I'm good at it, and I feel a sense of accomplishment when I kill bad people. The first few times it was a bit scary; then it was exciting; then it became a job."

Donny's eyes never left the four girl's playing on the monkey bars. His mind locked to them as if their presence and happiness gave him the strength to go on.

"But now, I feel damaged, Lisa. Like a part of my soul was wounded and had to be cauterized to reconcile and save my humanity. I don't enjoy killing, and I don't want to do it anymore. But the sad truth is this: it's what I do best and it's what the world needs most. Especially now."

Lisa let that sink in. She wanted to say something but everything crossing her mind rang hollow to her. All of a sudden she felt shallow and selfish.

"I'm sorry I feel this way, Donny. It's probably not fair to you but …" Donny interrupted her.

"I need to be around decent people like you and Samantha. I need to be reminded of why I'm doing this. I need to know that someday, when all this is over, I'll be able to put it aside and return to the rest of the human race, that I can be normal again. And maybe … just maybe … someone can love me and I can love them back. I don't want to kill. I want to create."

Lisa sat on the park bench dumbfounded. She'd always hated his arrogance and bravado, his smooth talk and cocky smile. But now, he seemed almost like a little boy who'd fallen and skinned his knee on the playground who needed holding. And she was a nurse.

She looked out at her daughter and tears welled up in her eyes. In her heart, Lisa knew that her daughter was allowed to play and laugh and run with other children, simply because of people like Donny Brewster who were willing to put their humanity on hold, to face their inner demons, to give up a piece of their soul in order for others to live and enjoy some measure of freedom and happiness. Before the Battle of Iroquois County, she'd always taken that for granted.

Lisa turned her blue eyes toward Donny, and their eyes locked together. She reached out and touched his hand. The feeling of electricity ebbed into his skin, and he tensed.

"I can't be what you want, Donny, but I can give you what you need."

Her eyes had softened, but Donny's took on a confused stare.

"Are you saying you want to have sex with me?"

Lisa's eyes turned to fire as she pulled her hand away from his.

"You idiot! Why do you always ruin moments like this!? Why do you always screw up these tender moments?"

Donny shrugged.

"I don't know. I'm a man."

Lisa jumped up off the bench and started to walk away. Donny just sat there, afraid to say anything else. He thought it odd that he found it easy to march into battle tomorrow, to face impossible odds, to attack superior forces, to shove a knife into a man's guts and hold onto him as the life drained away, to kill or be killed, but … this five foot five blonde who couldn't beat him in arm wrestling just scared the hell out of him.

Lisa stopped and turned around abruptly.

"Listen, do you want me to be your friend or not!?"

Donny thought for a moment, then quickly nodded his head. "Yeah, sure."

"Good. Okay then. Go to war tomorrow. Kill lots of bad guys. And when you get back we can grill hamburgers at my place and talk about it. Okay?"

"Sure. Sounds good."

And then she picked up Samantha and walked away from the playground. Sergeant Donny Brewster, highly trained master sniper, killer of hundreds of men, softly smiled, all the while realizing that in head-to-head combat, he was no match for Lisa Vanderboeg and her five-year-old daughter.

Dan Branch Goes to War

"BUT WHY DO YOU HAVE TO GO WITH DONNY TO SOME super-secret invasion just because Uncle Rodney wants you to?"

Dan knew it was a losing argument and one he'd best not perpetuate. "I don't know, honey. I just got this call from Colonel MacPherson, and he's sending down a helicopter for Donny and I."

There was a breeze on the porch this morning, and a lock of her coarse, black hair blew down into her eyes. Jackie brushed it away with more annoyance than the situation merited. She wasn't going to tell Dan this, but, if truth be told, she was upset because she didn't like being left behind. Baby Donna, now six months old was playing in a sand box just off the porch.

"What is this mission all about?"

"I don't know, honey. I'll be briefed when we get to where ever we're going."

Dan reached over and touched her shoulder, but she moved it away like his fingers were poison.

"Don't touch me, Dan Branch!"

It usually meant trouble when she used his full name. Dan wasn't a stupid man in most things, but when it came to a woman and her feelings, he felt no smarter than Forrest Gump, just like the rest of the male race. A part of him wanted to throw up his hands and just give up, but the other part of him, the part that loved her and wanted a future, knew enough to hang in there until this storm blew over.

"Honey, why don't you just tell me what's wrong. I hate it when you try to make me guess. I'm not that smart. Just open up your mouth and tell me straight out why you're mad that I'm going on a top secret mission for Uncle Rodney."

And then it hit him.

"Oh my – oh my. I think I've got it."

She looked at him like he was crazy.

"You don't have anything. You're just talking."

Dan smiled.

"Yes I do. I know what's bothering you. You want to come with me, don't you?"

Jackie turned her gaze away to the west.

"No. You're a stupid man. Just go away."

Dan smiled and moved closer to her.

"I wish you could come with me. I really do, but I don't think we should be taking the baby into a dangerous situation like that. I have no idea what I'm heading off into. It could be a shooting war for all I know."

Dan placed his hand on her shoulder, and this time she didn't pull away.

"I just don't understand why the men get to have all the fun. You get to train and fight wars and go off on wild super-secret adventures while I'm stuck home breast feeding and cleaning dirty diapers. Why can't you stay home and take care of the baby while I go on the mission?"

A blank look came over Dan's face, then he reached down with his free hand and rubbed back and forth along his pectoral muscles as if looking for something.

"I don't know, honey. I keep waiting, but my milk hasn't

come in yet."

Jackie tried to stifle a smile but couldn't hold it back. Dan turned her toward him and wrapped both his arms around her, bringing her in close.

"I love you, Jackie. Isn't that enough?"

She buried her face into his chest, was silent for a moment and then sobbed.

"I don't know what's wrong with me, Dan. I'm not like the other women. I work with them every day, and they just all seem to be content watching their men march off to war while they sit home taking care of kids."

She moved her head back and then looked up into his eyes imploringly.

"What's wrong with me, honey?"

Dan smiled and looked into her dark eyes sympathetically. He grabbed a handful of her black, Lebanese hair and let it run through his fingers like grains of sand dropping onto the beach.

"It's because you're special. You married into a strange family. Your father-in-law is the commanding general of the Shadow Militia; your husband is a colonel, and we're living in dangerous times, where any of us could die without a moment's notice."

He put his right hand on the back of her head and pulled it into his muscled chest. He gently stroked the back of her head as he spoke.

"You're special, honey. You're a Branch."

Jackie wrapped her arms around his waist and squeezed as hard as she could.

"I'm not going to let you go, Dan Branch."

Dan smiled and thought to himself. *I love this woman, but keeping her under control is like roping the wind.*

Baby Donna looked up at them and laughed as she shoved another handful of dirt into her mouth.

CHAPTER 7

The Blind Man's Bluff?

JARED THOMPSON LOOKED UP AT Sammy Thurmond, who was standing beside the couch, waiting dutifully as his boss studied the autopsy report he'd just been handed. He always hated giving The Blind Man bad news, but, at the same time, it always interested him as to how his boss would handle it. In over fifteen years of crises, complications and complex plans gone awry, Sammy Thurmond had never seen his boss visibly upset. Jared Thompson was always in control of himself and the environment around him.

It took a full five minutes, but, eventually, Jared looked up from the paper and stared at the wall in front of him. Then he placed the report down on the coffee table and thought some more. Finally, he crossed his legs and leaned back as he spoke. His voice had the same edge of calm it always had.

"So there was a tracking device embedded in Major Danskill's right buttocks. Interesting. Very interesting."

He didn't know how it had happened, whether Danskill had known about it, or, had even collaborated in the venture, but, seeing as though Danskill was dead, it probably no longer mattered. Jared now realized he'd made a mistake in killing him so quickly. In retrospect, he should have first extracted as much information as possible. He would have to examine that further.

"We'll have to make it a matter of policy to scan everyone in the future before we bring them to the facility. However, that makes no difference now."

Sammy thought he sensed a violent edge to The Blind Man's voice.

"I want you to prepare for an attack. Triple the Combat Air Patrol and extend it out to a two hundred mile radius." Jared reached up and scratched his chin with his left hand, and then placed both hands in his lap.

"And reduce the ground-level perimeter security personnel by two-thirds. I want just a few armed security up top. Stage our special forces listening posts every five hundred yards out to five miles in all directions. They are to observe and report only. Do not engage.

"Place a combat-ready swift reactionary force of one thousand men on standby. Have twenty Apaches ready to fly at all times, but only two should be in the air until I give the command to do otherwise. Reroute the satellites so that I have real-time intelligence. I want to know the moment his troops enter the area."

The Blind Man hesitated, as if contemplating the seriousness of his next decision. He didn't want to admit it, but he was consumed with the idea of killing Rodney T Branch, not just killing him, but torturing him and destroying all he held dear. "And move all our infantry and armored reserves to within seven miles east of the compound. Tell them to prepare for counterattack. Divide them into three groups, and they should be ready to move at a moment's notice."

Jared was simultaneously angered and challenged by the fact his location had been compromised by the Shadow Militia. While the prospect of an attack excited him, he wanted to make sure he was ready for it and that he always maintained the edge. In the back of his mind, he kept reminding himself, *General Rodney T Branch has never lost a fight. Behave accordingly. Give him the respect he deserves – and then kill him. Never underestimate the Shadow Militia ever again.*

"And one other thing. Pack up my things and move them to the secondary headquarters. I don't want to take any unnecessary chances."

As usual, Sammy Thurmond showed no emotion, but, deep inside, hidden and protected, he began to harbor second thoughts.

Escanaba, Michigan

COLONEL MACPHERSON HAD JUST FINISHED LAYING OUT the battle plans for the coming attack on the hardened, underground facility in Pennsylvania. He walked back to his seat now. First, he'd gone over the ground assault which included ten thousand light infantry troops from Michigan, Pennsylvania, Ohio, West Virginia and New Hampshire. They would all converge simultaneously on the target and arrive mere hours before the attack launched. Second, had been the air attack. This included F-16 fighters for air cover as well as A-10 Warthogs and Apache helicopter gunships to ward off any counterattack.

General Branch stepped up to the podium and looked out at the fifty or so men and women seated before him. His nephew, Colonel Dan Branch was seated in the front row alongside Sergeant Donny Brewster, and Colonel MacPherson. General Masbruch, the commanding officer of Shadow Militia, Eastern Command, was also there with his Chief of Staff, Lieutenant Colonel Samuelson.

"Brothers and sisters in arms, friends, soldiers and patriots. I don't have to tell you what's riding on this one battle. Due to the ingenuity of Colonel MacPherson and a few high-tech toys, we've been handed the opportunity of a lifetime.

"We have the chance to end this war with one fierce, strong and vicious attack. Within forty-eight hours, if all goes well, this war will be over."

The dead silence was broken by people turning in their chairs to make eye contact with those sitting beside them. Some even spoke in hushed whispers. The excitement was obvious. General Branch waited a moment before raising his hand to restore military order. His officers immediately silenced.

"Because of this unique opportunity, I've decided to merge both of Colonel MacPherson's plans into one. We will launch a coordinated air and ground attack in less than forty-eight hours with everything we have. I hate to risk all our assets in one battle, but this is a formidable adversary and we'll need all our resources to accomplish the mission."

The silence in the room seemed to get louder. No one spoke or even moved. Finally, General Masbruch stood to his feet and began to clap. The other officers, one by one, stood up as well and joined in, and, within a few seconds, the entire room was on its feet and cheering.

General Branch smiled. For better or worse; they were ready for battle.

As everyone filed out of the briefing room, the senior officer made his way out of the building and walked a full two blocks away before stopping in an alley. There was another meeting in thirty minutes, so he had to make this quick. He pulled out his cell phone, which, wasn't really a cell phone at all, but a high-tech satellite phone. He punched in the number and waited. Finally, a voice on the other end came on the line.

"What do you have for me?"

"I have to be brief. The attack is on. All Shadow Militia forces of both air and ground will converge on your location in forty-eight hours."

There were a few seconds of silence.

"Excellent. Thank you for your superior service, Colonel …"

"No names. I told you no names!"

The Blind Man laughed softly to himself.

"Of course. I understand."

"It's risky for me to pass information on to you, so I'll only contact you again if there are any changes."

"As you wish, Mr. X. And once again, thank you."

Jared put the satphone down on the coffee table, carved from a rare jungle tree and stolen from a now-deceased Columbian drug lord. He took off his sun glasses and looked around at the sprawling bungalow. It was lavish and ornate with all the comforts of home. He was going to miss it.

RODNEY BRANCH WAS SITTING IN THE HIGH-BACKED chair, looking across Mac's old, oak desk, wondering if he was doing the right thing. If he was correct, then the Shadow Militia would be saved, and the cause would survive, giving hope for freedom to the next generation. If he was wrong, then the enemy of freedom would be given a new lease on life, and this war would go on for years to come. The cost of human life would be great.

Sitting across from him were Colonel Dan Branch, Sergeant Donny Brewster and General Masbruch. Colonel MacPherson was standing up in the corner with his arms across his chest, his back ramrod stiff, peering out with eyes like blue granite.

General Branch was the first to speak. He decided to start out light, and then move into the difficult news.

"So, Sergeant Brewster, how are things going with that young nurse of yours? Any further news to report?"

The young sergeant seemed a bit taken aback, surrounded by colonels and generals, the lowly non-com felt out of place. Normally confident and sure, his voice wavered a bit as he answered his general.

"Well, sir, it's too soon to say. All I can report is initial resistance is strong, but that Marines don't surrender, and I will continue to press the attack."

Rodney nodded and smiled. He liked the boy.

"Rodney, did you actually call me in here to talk about this man's love life? Because I've got a mission to execute, probably the most important battle I'll ever fight."

Rodney looked over at the only other general in the room. This wasn't going to be easy.

"Actually, Dale, that's what I need to talk to you about." He hesitated as if choosing his words carefully. "I have a new mission for you."

General Dale Masbruch cocked his head to one side. "Excuse me?"

Rodney smiled, but then his face grew stern and deadly serious.

"The attack plans that Mac drew up are flawless and sheer genius. But there's a problem."

General Masbruch sighed but said nothing.

"We don't have the resources to execute it."

Dan Branch looked over at Donny, who returned his gaze. General Masbruch locked eyes with Rodney.

"Then why the hell are we doing this!?"

Rodney looked down at the desk, then brought up his hands and folded them atop the oak. He suddenly felt ten years older and very, very tired.

"Because we are weak, and we need to appear strong."

General Masbruch almost lifted himself off the chair, but forced himself to remain seated.

"For god's sake, Rodney, we're on the cusp of life or death of a culture and you're quoting me Sun Tzu? Just spit it out, man! What are we doing?"

Colonel MacPherson stepped forward. "General Branch, if I may?"

Rodney nodded and leaned back in his chair.

"We have a traitor in our senior command structure, and those of you in this room are the only ones to be trusted. When we reach the enemy headquarters in Pennsylvania every person we send will be attacked and annihilated, because our enemy has all the details of our battle plan. Aside from that, we don't possess a sufficient number of battle-ready F-16s and pilots or even A-10 Warthogs to successfully complete this mission. And we certainly don't have ten thousand troops to employ in battle."

He paused a moment before going on. He saw the large, green vein pulsing on General Masbruch's forehead and wondered if it was going to spring a leak.

"If The Blind Man knew exactly how weak we really are, then he would simply move in and crush us. We need to buy some time to build up and train an army. We need time to transform farmers and factory workers into battle-ready fighters. We need to create supply chains, and manufacture weaponry. We have to train and equip an army using nothing but the skeleton command of the Shadow Militia. That's our only chance. And, quite frankly, has been the plan from day one. 'Appear strong when you are weak, and weak when you are strong.'"

Colonel Dan Branch who had been silent up until now, finally broke in. "So who is The Blind Man?"

Colonel MacPherson stepped back into the corner, and Rodney took over again. "The Blind Man is our enemy, and he has us outgunned, outmanned, and outsupplied. He has most of the technological capabilities of the former United States government. And here's how we're going to beat him."

Rodney talked on for a full half hour, outlining details and plans, all the while, General Masbruch's pulsing forehead began to subside.

CHAPTER 8

Attack of the Black Flies

"What do you think, Mac?" Colonel MacPherson stared into the computer screen, watching the two lone guards pacing back and forth in front of the pole barn set into the side of the Pennsylvania mountain. They were in digital camo, with M4s hanging from one-point slings in front of them.

"I think you're right, sir. It's a trap."

General Branch reached up to stroke his chin with his left hand, and he continued to rub his thumb and forefinger along the sides of his cheeks in heavy contemplation.

"This guy's good, Mac. I'll give him that. He knows we have located his headquarters, and he also realizes how we found it. Which means he now knows something more about us and our capabilities. That's unfortunate. I liked it better when we were just a myth in the shadows."

Colonel MacPherson, who was seated beside the general picked up his coffee cup, blew away the steam and took a sip. "We could just back away, melt off into the shadows again, and live to fight another day."

Rodney got up and walked over to the coffee pot. He poured himself another cup before standing off to one side of the window and peering out into the Upper Peninsula June sky. The black flies would be out soon, and they'd be driving them all crazy with their terrible little bites. That's what they were to The Blind Man, just tiny little black flies, buzzing around his head, and making him mad. Rodney turned back to his colonel and smiled.

"We have to keep him guessing, Mac. We have to keep The Blind Man at an arm's length to give us more time to train and prepare for all-out war."

Rodney walked back to his chair and sat down again. He placed his coffee mug on the desk and began to trace circles with his forefinger around the rim of the cup. Colonel MacPherson tossed him a coaster and Rodney laughed out loud before placing the disk beneath his coffee cup.

"I think it's funny that you and I are planning the greatest war for freedom since the American revolution, and you still have time to worry about coffee stains on your desk."

Mac shrugged. "It's a nice desk."

"True. But it's still just a desk." He took a sip and burned his tongue. "I don't think he's going to underestimate us again, Mac. I think he's going to try and destroy us as soon as possible."

Mac looked over. "Meaning?"

"Meaning the time to look weak has come and gone. Now is the time to appear strong."

"Rodney, why do you talk in riddles so much and spend so much time thinking out loud. Just say what you mean."

Rodney liked it when Mac dropped the military formalities and addressed him more like a friend than a general.

"What is the heaviest, most powerful weapon we have in our arsenal?"

The colonel was taking a sip of his coffee, but he stopped and looked over at General Branch. "You can't be serious."

Rodney smiled. He put both elbows onto the desk and peered down into his coffee cup. "We have to do something, and the plan we've made is untenable. The worst thing we could do right now is to put forth an appearance of weakness. The Blind Man is beating us on all fronts. He's called in mercenaries from Europe and South America. We are running low on ammo and supplies all across America. We need to get his attention, to shake up the chess board a bit. Up until now he's felt invincible. I need The Blind Man to fear for his life."

Colonel MacPherson's military bearing returned as if it had never left. "But sir, we only have one."

General Branch nodded. "True, but The Blind Man doesn't know that. Besides, power is impotent without the resolve to use it." He took a sip of his coffee and placed the heavy mug back down. "And ... once the internet is back up and running, I'll just log on to Ebay and buy us some more."

The colonel scoffed. "Right, Ebay. You don't even have a credit card, Rodney."

Rodney laughed. "True, but my best friend has American Express."

Mac smiled and shook his head from side to side. He turned and looked out the window at the Upper Peninsula sunshine. He had a feeling life was about to pick up the pace.

Ten Miles West of Blind Man HQ

"JACKIE WAS PRETTY UPSET WHEN SHE FOUND OUT I WAS leaving on this mission."

Donny Brewster laughed out loud. "Of course she was upset! She's a woman! Women are crazy."

They were sitting on top of a mountain, on the edge of a rock cliff inside central Pennsylvania, looking out across a few lesser mountains to their objective. General Branch was conducting an air strike on The Blind Man's headquarters, and their orders were strictly to observe and report from due east of the target. Under no circumstances were they to approach within ten miles. Dan and Donny had both secretly wondered what they could possibly see from ten miles out, but both assumed they'd be told to move closer when the time was right. There was a small cave just a few yards to their right where they had stowed the quads. It was a sunny day and upwards of eighty degrees, and Donny and Dan, dressed in woodland camo, were already sweating profusely. If not for the strong wind coming out of the west, it would be a very uncomfortable day.

"So what do you know about women anyways. You've never been married have you?"

"Nope, never made that mistake."

Colonel Dan Branch smiled. "But I notice you've been spending a little time with Nurse Vanderboeg again. How is that going?"

Sergeant Brewster grunted. "Huh. It's going. I guess. I just don't understand women."

Dan took a drink from his olive drab canteen and put it on the ground beside him. "Well, she's a beautiful woman. So, whatever she's done, I suppose you'll have to forgive her."

Donny grinned at the colonel, showing a whole mouthful of teeth. "Why are us men such suckers for good looking women? They wiggle their butts, and we just follow them around like little, lost puppy dogs, no matter what kind of emotional hell they put us through."

Dan laughed. "I don't know. I imagine it has something to do with too much testosterone. Whatever it is, I hope I never outgrow it."

They were both lying on their stomachs in the dirt, and Donny rolled to one side to look Dan in the eyes. "Really? Do you think it's worth all the effort then?"

Without a moment's hesitation, Dan showed his own teeth and answered. "Absolutely, Marine. I would die for that woman, and I'm hoping you can find a lady of your own worth dying for."

Dan rolled over onto his back and looked up at the clear, blue sky. "Yup. Donny, I'll be honest with you. A good woman like Jackie is worth her weight in Mocha flavored Frappuccino."

Donny rolled over on his back and burst out laughing. "Wow! That good, huh?" A few seconds later he stopped and moved back onto his stomach before reaching over to his right. He started digging into his back pack for something.

"I almost forgot. I found this at that abandoned gas station a few miles back." He pulled out a clear glass bottle filled with dirty, brown liquid. Dan recognized it immediately.

"Holy cow! It's a Mocha Frappuccino! Is it mine?"

Donny tossed it down into the dirt like it meant nothing to him. "I wouldn't drink that stuff if my life depended on it. It's all yours, Colonel."

Dan held it in his left palm, and ran the fingers of his right hand over the plastic label. "I haven't had a Frappuccino since …" And then his voice stopped.

"What's wrong?"

Dan shrugged. "Nothing. I was just thinking of the last time I had one of these. It was the night I met Jackie."

Sergeant Brewster sat up and took a look around the perimeter. He wasn't usually so lax on a mission, but he had claymores set up all around them, with only one dirt road to access their position. Both men relaxed and lay flat on their backs, looking up into the blue sky of mid-day.

"So spill it, Marine. Talk to me."

A serious look came over Dan as he spoke. His voice had taken on a subdued tone. "It was the day after I'd killed my first man … well, five men actually. Jeremy and I were camped in the woods by a stream in Northeast Wisconsin. I was reading the Bible and drinking Frappuccino cooled in the creek. Then Jeremy and I had a good talk, the first good one in a long time. We went to bed and woke up to a woman screaming. It was Jackie. She'd been kidnapped – her and her husband. I followed her, then killed the three men holding them." He stopped. Donny waited patiently.

"But I accidentally shot her husband as well. I wish I could take that shot back. But, if I did, well, then I wouldn't have her. It's a real cluster."

Donny was about to answer when he felt the ground shake beneath him. Almost immediately after the rumble they heard the explosion. Both men glanced up, almost at the same time, and took in the pillar of black and orange cloud rising up ten miles to their eastern flank.

"Holy shit!"

For a few seconds they stared in awe with mouths dropped wide open. Then Dan jumped up and ran to the cave where their quads were hidden. Donny was right behind him. Once inside they moved to the back wall, and huddled in the dark, waiting for the sound of the explosion to die away.

Over the fading sound of the detonation, Dan heard a tiny snap. The large glow stick lit up the small cave in a green iridescent glow. They were thirty feet back from the mouth of the cave with both quads behind them. Dan was the first to speak.

"Donny ... was that a nuke?"

Sergeant Brewster nodded his head in the dim light, all the while struggling to remember the details of his NBC training from the Marine Corps.

"Are we far enough away, Dan?"

"I think so. It depends on how many kilotons it was. If that was the objective, then we're ten miles from ground zero, and we've got about a fifteen-mile-an-hour wind blowing straight from the west. Plus, this cave should give us pretty good protection, provided it doesn't fall down on our heads."

Donny sat flat on his butt and leaned his back against the quad's rear tire. "That was different than all the nuclear blasts I've seen on television. It was a lot louder."

Dan nodded in the green light. "Yeah, and it was weird the way we felt the ground shake before we heard the blast."

"Colonel, I say we wait a bit and then get the hell outta Dodge."

Dan nodded. "I like the way you non-coms think. Let's see

if the radio still works, then we can call this in, give our report and then put some clicks between us and Mr. Atom."

Donny glanced over at the quads. "What about them – the EMP – will they even start?"

Dan nodded. "I think so. They were inside the cave pretty far shielded by solid rock." He forced a smile on his face. "I guess we'll find out 'eh Marine?"

Donny smiled back nervously before answering. "Uh, yeah. I guess so." He looked around him for the radio, but it was nowhere to be found. "So, which one of us is going out there to get the radio?"

Dan's smile spread even larger. "Well, *Sergeant* Brewster. *Colonel* Branch thinks it should be you."

Donny's face clouded over. "You're going to pull rank on me after all we've been through? I thought we were friends."

"Of course we're friends. It's not my fault I have an uncle in high places."

All of a sudden Donny threw his head back and burst out laughing. Dan's face grew stern.

"What's so funny, Marine?"

After calming himself down, Donny said, "We left your Frappuccino outside, and it is now radioactive!"

Colonel Branch buried his head in his hands. "I don't believe this. The last Frappuccino on the planet was just destroyed by a nuclear bomb!"

The Blind Man - Alternate Headquarters

JARED THOMPSON WATCHED THE BIG SCREEN ROIL AND boil as the black cloud mushroomed up into the air, atomizing and dispersing the now incinerated personnel and contents of his state-of-the art military headquarters. He guessed it to be a tactical nuke of about ten kilotons. For a brief moment he thought, *That could have been me.* But he quickly shook off the feeling of vulnerability.

Without thinking, The Blind Man slammed his wine goblet

down on the beautiful coffee table, stolen from the now-deceased Columbian drug lord. The goblet shattered into a hundred pieces. Jared turned his back on the screen and rubbed his eyes with his left hand. He'd just lost his headquarters and thousands of soldiers, many of them irreplaceable Special Forces. Quickly, he regained his composure, and softly issued orders to his right-hand man.

"Mr. Thurmond, please gather as much intel as possible from the air and from any surviving forces on the ground. I would like to know what happened and how. Can you do that for me, please, Mr. Thurmond?"

Sammy Thurmond's stone-cold face betrayed no emotion, but inside he was secretly vexed. He doubted very much if anyone on the ground would survive the blast and ensuing radiation, which meant this was a major loss for The Blind Man.

He curtly nodded and bowed slightly before quickly exiting the room. It was a stunning revelation to see his boss was no longer in complete control.

Escanaba HQ

Former CIA Agent Jeff Arnett sat across the table from his new boss, General Rodney Branch. Jeff had met many powerful men in his day, but none quite like Rodney. In Jeff's summation, most powerful men contained obvious flaws: either arrogance, selfishness or maybe greed or just plain brutality. But he still hadn't pinpointed the general's major flaw. The general was the first to speak.

"I need you to help me kill twenty-five-thousand Islamists."

Jeff was a tall man, and he made the chair he was sitting in appear smaller than it really was.

"Why?"

"Because they need killing, and I can't do it on my own. You know things I don't. You have the benefit of experience that I need to draw on. That's why we recruited you in the first place."

Jeff cocked his head to one side and smiled. "You recruited me? I thought I came to you."

General Branch shrugged. "Semantics. Who cares. You're here and I need your help."

Jeff watched as the general's right hand reached up to the left-breast pocket of his camo utility shirt. It stopped halfway and came back down. Special Agent Arnett immediately deduced the truth. Either the general had recently stopped smoking or just ran out of cigarettes. Jeff found that interesting and filed it away for future reference.

"Do you hate Muslims, General Branch?"

Rodney shrugged his shoulders and leaned back in his chair. "On a case-by-case basis, sure. For example, I hate the twenty-five-thousand of them who are marching this way and want to kill me." The general took a sip of his coffee and placed it firmly back down on the desk. "To be more precise about it, it's not that I hate them. I just don't trust them."

Jeff crossed his right leg over his left. "So why don't you trust them?"

Rodney looked at the man blankly. "I don't trust anyone who's trying to kill me."

Jeff smiled without thinking. That was unusual for him. "How about me? Do you trust me?"

"No."

"Why not?"

"Because you're asking me stupid questions and trying to psychoanalyze me and I don't like people getting into my head. It gives them power I don't want them to have. I am what I am and that's that. You can either like it or not like it. I really don't care. But right now I'd like you to stop wasting my time and help me figure out a way to kill these ragheads."

Jeff was amazed. He'd never met anyone so black and white. He thought for a moment. Rodney Branch intrigued him, and he liked that. He came to a decision and nodded.

"Sure. How can I help?"

Rodney leaned forward and placed his elbows on the desk.

"I want you to tell me everything you know about Abdul Al'Kalwi. I want to know everything about Islam. I want to know the culture: what they eat, how they dress, how they think about everything. And, most importantly, I want to know how I can piss them off."

Jeff smiled again. He was really starting to like this man. By pre-The-Day standards, he was blunt to the point of rudeness, but he spoke his mind in a simple and matter-of-fact way.

"Okay then. Let's start by talking about the history of Islam, how it started, all about Mohammed. Then we'll move on to the culture of the Middle East and then Abdul Al'Kalwi." He uncrossed his legs and sat up straight. "Can I get a more comfortable chair, though, because this is going to take a really long time."

Uncle Rodney laughed out loud, and Agent Arnett was taken aback by the suddenness of the outburst.

"Yeah, sure. Let's go into the other room." The two men got up and left Colonel MacPherson's office to begin the first of many multi-hour discussions on Islam and the Middle East culture.

CHAPTER 9

__Iroquois City__

"That son of a bitch really does have nukes?! I don't believe it!"

Sheriff Joe Leif sat at the kitchen table of his house across from Colonel Dan Branch. Both were drinking coffee and eating corn bread made by Joe's wife, Marge.

"Joseph Grant Leif! Now you watch your language! I won't tolerate that in my house."

Marge Leif's fierce gray eyes glared down at her husband as she wiped her wet hands on a cotton apron tied to her front.

"Sorry honey. It just slipped out."

Marge turned back to her dishwater in the sink. "Seems like it's been slipping out more often than necessary these days." Her hands moved in the sink, and Dan Branch could hear the dishes clank together as she washed them.

"This is great corn bread, Marge. You should give the recipe to Jackie. I think she'd like it too."

Marge stopped washing and turned around to answer him. Her original sweet demeanor had returned. "Why thank you, Dan. I'll send it home with you." Then she turned back to her dishes as if the world depended on it. Joe and Dan continued their conversation.

"You should have seen it, Joe. Donny and I were only ten miles away and the ground shook before we even heard the explosion. I was surprised at that, but Rodney told me it's because shock waves travel through the ground faster than through the air."

Joe took a sip of his coffee. "I didn't know that."

"Neither did I. But we didn't know Uncle Rodney had nukes either."

"There's a lot we didn't know about your Uncle Rodney. Seems that old man just keeps on surprising us." Joe looked at the kitchen wall and stroked his chin. "I wonder where he got all that stuff. I know darn well it's wasn't from Ebay. So where's he at now?"

Dan finished swallowing his corn bread before answering. "I don't know for sure. I guess he's somewhere on the east coast, maybe New Hampshire. He's been traveling all over the country trying to rally the troops and get them better trained and equipped."

"Rally the troops? Rally them against who?"

"Some guy he calls The Blind Man."

"The Blind Man?"

Dan brushed crumbs off his lightly starched olive drab fatigues. "Yup. He seems to think he's public enemy number one. I guess this guy has usurped the lion's share of power on the East and West coasts, and now he's trying to pacify middle America."

"So what makes Rodney so sure this guy's the bad guy?"

Dan shrugged. "I don't know. I didn't ask. But have you ever known my uncle to be wrong in the past eight months, especially about military things?"

"Guess not." Joe sipped his coffee again. "Marge, honey, can I get a refill?"

Marge sighed and dried her hands before moving to the coffee pot. She refilled first her husband's cup and then Dan's. Dan had set the Leif family up with a limited number of car batteries and solar trickle chargers to give them certain luxuries like coffee pots and lamps. It was a pain in the butt to recharge and move them around, but it was better than living in the stone age.

"So, did the Doc check you out? You're not sterilized or anything from the radiation are you?"

Dan laughed out loud. "No. We were inside a cave and beat feet outta there pretty fast. We weren't there long enough to absorb a lot of radiation. It helps we were 10 miles upwind. Jackie was worried about the same thing. She's a bit mad at Rodney for sending me to watch a nuclear bomb go off."

Marge let the water out of the sink as she spoke. "Well, you can't really blame her for that." All the water for drinking, bathing and for cooking had to be hauled in from the creek a hundred yards from the house. The Leif's were on a waiting list to have a hand pump well driven to replace the useless electric well they now had.

"So what's going to happen now, Dan? Does Rodney know?"

Dan shook his head. "Maybe. Maybe not. You know my Uncle Rodney. Mr. Mysterious. He might know, but he sure as …" And then he caught himself before swearing. He glanced at Marge, but she wasn't smiling. "I mean he probably knows but isn't telling me anything. That's just the way he is. He just keeps pushing me to strengthen the county alliances and expand them. We're training soldiers like I never thought possible. Just like Rodney's traveling around the country, I'm traveling around northern Michigan. We added three more counties just yesterday. They sent delegations to us, asking to be part of the mutual defense pact."

"Really?"

"Yup. Everyone wants to be allied with the biggest kid on the block, and, right now, that's Uncle Rodney."

Joe shifted in his chair to cross one leg over the other. "Well, that's true. He is the only nuclear power in northern Michigan that we know of."

Marge Leif abruptly changed the subject. "So, Dan, when are you and Jackie going to get pregnant?"

Dan turned to her and smiled. He liked her blunt, direct approach. People always knew what Marge Leif was thinking, whether they wanted to or not.

From there the conversation transitioned to the rigors of daily life. There was a market in town set up at the city park. Some people paid using silver, others paid in bullets, but most people used a system of barter. Some people had been concerned that Sheriff Leif would impose a consumption tax, but Joe had quickly squelched that rumor. "No sense in re-creating the mistakes of the past in rebuilding the new world," he'd said. "As long as I'm in charge, there will be no taxes, just mutual support and cooperation." The people had liked that and commerce began to flourish in Iroquois county, bringing in traders from across the north. Joe had a staff of ten deputies now who helped him keep the peace, but Dan Branch and his Home Guard bore the brunt of the county's border defense.

Dan and Donny continued to recruit and train soldiers. Beginners were taught basic skills, while veteran warriors continued on their journey to becoming snipers, recon scouts, demolition experts, guerilla warriors or whatever else was needed. Iroquois county, not through choice, but through necessity, had become the regional power of the North. And with power came a certain measure of stability.

The Blind Man's New HQ

JARED THOMPSON LOOKED UP AT THE BIG SCREEN. HE pushed a few buttons on the laptop and manipulated the maps a bit more until he had what he wanted. He had been thinking about only one man for the past two days now, and his obsession with General Rodney T Branch worried him. At first, he'd wanted to strike back immediately with overwhelming force. He'd considered turning Escanaba into a smoking pile of radioactive ash, but had caught himself. *What would that accomplish? It would merely reduce the size of my empire.* And what if General Branch traded him nuke for nuke? What then? Jared knew the answer was unacceptable. The crazy doctrine of Mutual Assured Destruction was as sane and pragmatic now as it had been during the Cold War. Unless he knew for sure how many nukes General Branch had and where they were deployed … no, that was not the answer.

He knew he had to regain control of the situation and of his emotions. He'd learned from past mistakes that obsessions were a weakness and could prove his undoing. He'd have to kill General Branch, but his pride and his anger would have to take a back seat to rational, well thought out military strategy.

Every problem has a solution, and usually the solution is already embedded in the problem itself. He just had to analyze it and see it for what it was. Jared went back to the beginning and summarized his problem at a most basic level.

Pacification in the South was moving ahead, but behind schedule. Those damn rebel rednecks … No! He caught himself and started over, this time without the emotion. He spoke out loud to lend a feeling of realness and accountability.

"I'm behind schedule in the South. I'm ahead of schedule on the east and west coasts. The Muslim horde is conquering lower Michigan and moving against Chicago. The Rocky Mountain rebels are still resisting fiercely. The Shadow Militia is the head of the snake. General Branch lives in northern Michigan. Conquer Michigan and you kill the snake, then all else will fall into place."

Good. So now I have a clear objective. But how to achieve it.

"I have no forces in Michigan now that Major Danskill is gone. I have assets in Ohio, but they are occupied. I could hire and ship in more mercenaries from Central and South America, but that takes time, and, quite frankly, they suck as soldiers."

He sat down on the plush, Corinthian leather couch and reached out for his wine goblet. Most of his best wine had been irradiated by General Branch. His emotions rose up again, but he closed his eyes and quickly beat them back down. *Control. I need control to maintain clarity of thought.*

"In Michigan I have two problems: The Shadow Militia and the Muslim horde." The Blind Man cocked his head to one side and repeated to himself. "In Michigan I have two problems: The Shadow Militia and the Muslim horde." He took a sip of his wine. "Interesting. The Muslim horde. The Shadow Militia."

Suddenly, Jared smiled. He lifted his hand in a beckoning manner toward Sammy Thurmond, who had been waiting quietly in the far corner, waiting to do the will of his master. Sammy moved closer and patiently hovered a few feet away.

"Mr. Thurmond. I want all the information we have on Supreme General Abdul Al'Kalwi within thirty minutes. I want satellite photos. I want history, childhood, everything. I want a personality profile, his strengths and weaknesses. I want it all."

Jared flicked his hand and Sammy scooted off through the door. The Blind Man's whole countenance suddenly changed. He took another sip of his wine. Yes, within every problem is embedded its own solution. Thoroughly understand the problem, and the solution reveals itself.

Jackson, Michigan

SUPREME GENERAL ABDUL AL'KALWI LOOKED OUT over the alfalfa field. It was already eighteen inches high, and, on any other year prior to The Day, it would have been through its first hay cutting already. But there was no gas to run the tractors, so the hay continued to grow unabated. Nature was reclaiming its hold, and people were starving everywhere; it's not that there was no food, just no way to run the equipment to grow, fertilize, spray, and harvest the crops. Most farmers still had their land, and their families were eating well, because they could grow and harvest enough for their own consumption, but, the days of mechanized farming and corporate agriculture were over and would not return for many years to come, if ever. That was why Abdul was making special deals with the farmers. He was allowing them to keep their land in return for sixty percent of their crops. Abdul knew that food was the key to life, and life was the key to control. If he threatened a starving man with death, then he would readily accept death, and Abdul gained nothing. However, offer a starving man food, and he would accept it and pledge his fealty in return. Abdul had thought all this out. He'd even gone out of his way to gain control of all the seeds he could find. And heirloom seeds had been given a priority, because they, unlike hybrid seeds, were capable of creating more seed for the next year. So, all of lower Michigan was becoming his food belt, and he planned on doing the same to Indiana and Illinois. Once he had enough food to sustain the nation, then the once proud American people would kneel at his feet in return for their daily allotment of bread.

"Make camp here, but do not destroy the field. Hurry! It is almost time for evening prayer."

The Supreme General waved his hand and his underlings moved off quickly to do his bidding. He walked out into the alfalfa, feeling the green grass tickle his bare ankles and toes through his sandals. He removed his footwear and sat down in the hay field. It was a beautiful June day, the beginning of summer, and life was very good for Abdul Al'Kalwi and his army.

Things were going wrong, and his progress had been slowed considerably by all the cars blocking the interstate, but his new arrangement would fix all that. Allah had provided a way beyond his wildest dreams. As Abdul sat in the field and felt the breeze on his face, he readied his heart for prayer.

The Alfalfa Field - The Next Day

Supreme General Abdul Al'Kalwi looked up into the sky at the F-18 Hornet fighter jets racing above him. There were four of them, and they flew straight down in perfect wingtip-to-wingtip formation. They screamed down toward Abdul with deafening precision as he stood in the alfalfa field, once again in his bare feet. Thousands of his soldiers threw themselves to the ground in terror, but Abdul didn't move. He looked on in orgasmic anticipation as the jets made their pass, almost touching the earth before suddenly leveling out and beginning their near vertical climb back up into the sky.

That's when the Supreme General heard the helicopters coming in from the sunrise. He tried to count them, but there were too many. They were all gunships of some type, with machine guns and rockets beneath them. He smiled as the helicopters began to circle his encampment like angry wasps. Abdul had given orders that anyone firing at the aircraft would be tortured and executed. This turned out to be unnecessary as the sheer force of power had most of his men cowering in the dirt.

The larger helicopter moved in quickly and hovered over the alfalfa field. It slowly dropped down and cut its engine. Abdul watched as the rotors lost speed and eventually came to a stop. The door opened and the stairway dropped down. The Blind Man exited and walked slowly down the stairs followed closely by Sammy Thurmond. Sammy then moved to his master's side and led him toward the Supreme General who was meeting him halfway.

Jared was wearing his dark glasses and allowing himself to be led by his servant. When they merged in the field, Sammy Thurmond was the first to speak.

"The Supreme General is here, sir."

Jared smiled and offered a slight bow. Abdul didn't return it, but assumed a blind man wouldn't see it regardless. "Supreme General Al'Kalwi. It is a pleasure to meet such a fine military conqueror."

Abdul answered curtly. "Thank you."

For a clumsy moment there was silence, then the Supreme

General motioned to his tent about thirty yards away beside the field. "We may speak privately inside my quarters."

Abdul turned and walked slowly away, assuming he was being followed. As they went, he couldn't help but glance up at the sky, filled with military attack helicopters and fighter jets. They were the one thing he needed to make his dream of conquests come true. And now he had them.

The agreement had been simple. Abdul would rule all of Michigan's upper and lower peninsulas, but his ambitions for Indiana and Illinois must be ended. Abdul would agree to the terms, but had no intention of limiting his ambitions. He just had to placate the blind man, tell him what he wanted to hear, and then he'd be free to do as he pleased until he had enough power to bite the hand extended to him in friendship.

Jared smiled inside, but kept his poker face. He could smell the man's arrogance and lust for power. He was the perfect tool to crush the Shadow Militia. And, even if he failed to kill General Branch, at least he'd be weakened. With a little luck and clever manipulation, General Branch and General Al'Kalwi would meet on the field of battle, and Jared would emerge the winner.

CHAPTER 10

June 15th, Lansing, Michigan

SUPREME **G**ENERAL **A**L'**K**ALWI stood beneath the rotunda of the State Capitol in Lansing and looked straight up one-hundred and sixty feet to the peak of the large, multi-colored cast iron dome.

Michigan's first capitol had been in Detroit back in 1837 when Michigan became a state. That first building had been much smaller and more humble. The granite cornerstone for this present building had been laid in 1873 and boasted four main entrances facing north, south, east and west. The architecture was termed neo-classical, because it incorporated motifs from both Greek and Roman architecture, including Doric, Ionic and Corinthian columns.

Abdul looked around him at the huge marble columns and nodded his head in satisfaction. Yes, this would suffice as an office until more suitable arrangements could be made when he eventually attacked Chicago and other larger cities to the south and east.

According to his original battle plans, he had split his forces in Jackson, sending half to Lansing in the north and half to Kalamazoo in the west. As of today, both objectives had been taken and pacified. His standing army now numbered twenty-five thousand able-bodied men. He did not allow women to fight, as Islam considered them the weaker sex, and used them only for domestic chores, child-rearing and the sexual pleasures of men.

Now it was time to move on to Grand Rapids, the largest city in western Michigan, or, at least it had been the largest prior to The Day. Over the past nine months many had died, buildings destroyed and ravaged by roving gangs and smaller armies. Some of the city had burned to the ground. But Abdul would rebuild all the cities, and make them great again. As Abdul's army conquered, he always left a small garrison behind to restore order and to impose and maintain Sharia Law. The larger the city, the larger the garrison.

In his heart, he knew that most people, once they'd experienced the stability and strength of Islam, would appreciate his conquest and rule. He was doing it for them and for their progeny.

The addition of airpower had been a great boost to his military campaign in two ways. One, instead of scouting ahead on foot, he could send Apache helicopters to gather intelligence from the air. This told him in advance what he was facing in each town and told him how to deploy his troops with minimal losses. Second, people who saw the Apaches associated them with the federal government, and, thereby assumed help was on the way, along with food, medicine and other much-needed supplies. Of course, technically, that was true, just not in the way they anticipated. In some towns, he was welcomed as a liberating hero, albeit, not the hero they'd expected.

Because of this, his campaign was ahead of schedule. His only drawback was the low number of conscripts and converts. Almost everyone he came into contact with was willing to join his ranks, but most people had already died or moved off into the countryside, typically north. Abdul learned that a smaller gang-led force called The Horde had moved through west Michigan a few months before and decimated the population without regard to their well-being. However, Abdul would not make that mistake. He wanted loyal subjects for Allah; therefore, he would be a "kinder and gentler" despot, giving food and comfort to all who would accept it. Of course, there were stipulations. As traditional Americans had so universally once agreed, "There is no such thing as a free lunch." Abdul made his requirements clear and simple: submit to Allah and follow Sharia Law as the Supreme General saw fit … or die. Abdul considered his terms both reasonable and compassionate. Submission had been a small price to pay to Allah for centuries, and Abdul saw no reason to change a business model that had worked so well in the past.

The Supreme General took one last look around him, and then lifted his right hand and made a beckoning motion with his forefinger to no one in particular. Immediately, a servant was there.

"I want the speakers to begin the regular call to prayer, just as we have in the other cities. I want it done by afternoon prayer, or your head will drop to this beautiful rotunda floor. Understood?"

The servant nodded and bowed as he backed away. *Good*, he thought. Abdul didn't like misunderstandings.

Ten Days Later - Uncle Rodney's House

THE APACHE HELICOPTER HOVERED GENTLY OVER Uncle Rodney's house, whipping the newly leaf-covered trees into a frenzy. It descended slowly and touched down in his front yard. Dan, Sheriff Leif, Donny, Jeremy and Jackie and the baby stood clustered on the front deck watching. General Branch ducked his head down and stepped out onto the lawn. The grass was already a foot high. One of the benefits to the apocalypse was the absence of yard work, as no one was expected to mow their lawn anymore. Of course, Uncle Rodney had been one of the few nonconformists who hadn't mowed his lawn before The Day, so now his yard was considered normal for the first time.

Dan, Jeremy and Joe walked off the deck and moved out

to meet the general. Jackie and the baby looked on. Normally, Jackie would be smiling, but she already knew that something was wrong, and that it would bode ill for herself and her family. Dan walked in the lead as Sergeant Brewster kept to the left and slightly abreast of his colonel. Jeremy just seemed to be tagging along to the right of his father.

Dan and Donny stopped at attention. As the ranking officer, Dan gave his uncle a snappy Marine Corps salute. "Good afternoon, General Branch." Uncle Rodney looked at his nephew and smiled before returning the salute. Then he reached out and shook first Dan's hand then Joe Leif's and then Donny's. Rodney stopped when he reached Jeremy. The sixteen-year-old boy was rendering his best, untutored military salute. Uncle Rodney looked Jeremy in the eyes, and they seemed to twinkle in the sunlight, before their hard, granite-like countenance softened.

"Colonel Branch, please wait for me inside with the others. I'd like a few minutes with this young soldier."

Colonel Branch saluted, and Rodney returned it with military precision. Once they were alone, Rodney reached out and touched Jeremy's right hand, moving it into the proper shape and position. Then he placed his left hand under the boy's elbow and moved it parallel to the deck.

"When you salute, always stand at position of attention. Bring your heels together sharply on line, with your toes pointing out equally, forming a 45-degree angle. The weight of your body should be evenly on the heels and balls of both feet. Keep your legs straight without locking your knees, and hold your body erect with level hips, chest lifted and arched, and your shoulders square. Keep your head erect with pride and face straight to the front with the chin drawn in so that the alignment of your head and neck is vertical. Let your arms hang straight without stiffness. Curl your fingers so that the tips of the thumbs are alongside and touching the first joint of your forefingers. Keep your thumbs straight along the seams of your trouser leg with the first joint of the fingers touching your trousers."

Uncle Rodney made several other adjustments to Jeremy's body. Then he snapped himself to attention and returned the young man's salute.

"As you were, soldier. You can relax now, Jeremy. It's just me."

Jeremy's mouth broke into a grin. "I knew you'd come back, Uncle Rodney!"

General Branch laughed out loud and slapped the boy on his shoulders as they walked toward the house. Jackie was still on the porch with baby Donna who was now nine months old and soon to be a toddler. Jackie spoke with a tiny edge in her voice as soon as Rodney's feet touched the top wooden step.

"You're going to be sorely disappointed if you expect me to salute you, Uncle Rodney."

General Branch smiled as he held out his arms and the two embraced. Baby Donna's face was pressed against Rodney's olive drab, starched shirt. She slobbered on the perfectly pressed collar before the two adults separated.

"Jackie, I would be disappointed if you did salute. You know you're special."

Jackie smiled. "I know."

The general glanced over at Jeremy. "Head inside and join the other men, Jeremy. Let them know I'll be inside in a minute. I need to talk to Jackie for a few."

Jeremy snapped to attention and saluted crisply.

"Yes sir, General Branch!"

Rodney chuckled before returning the salute. Once Jeremy was inside and they were alone, Rodney wasted no time getting straight to the point.

"They all think I came here to meet specifically with them, but you and I are the only ones who know the whole truth. Did you keep the secret?"

Rodney reached over to take the baby while they talked.

"Yes, of course. Dan suspects nothing."

Uncle Rodney nodded. The baby reached up and dug her fingernails into the old man's face.

"It has to stay that way until we execute the plan. In the meantime you have to keep getting ready. It's dangerous, but I don't know what else to do, and there's no one else I can turn to on this. You are uniquely qualified."

Rodney kissed baby Donna and handed the baby back to her and then reached into the cargo pants pocket of his trouser leg. He pulled out several sheets of folded paper and handed them to her.

"Here's the latest intel on the situation. You need to study it. I'll be giving the others an overview, but you'll need all the info you can get. I'll keep sending updates to you as I get them."

Jackie smiled and looked down at the papers. She then reached up and pecked the old man on the cheek.

"Sure thing, Uncle Rodney." And then she shifted the baby to her left arm and gave the general her best salute. He laughed out loud, gave her a brief hug and then walked past her into the house.

Inside the kitchen, seated at the dining room table, Dan Branch fidgeted nervously in the chair. The table had four chromed legs with a red Formica top flecked with tiny gray dots. It was the same table Dan remembered as a child growing up in this house.

"Relax, Dan. Your nerves are tighter than a gnat's ass stretched over a barrel." Donny smiled slightly as he talked. "She'll be okay. Just like always. You need to stop underestimating her. Jackie can handle herself. Besides, the old man likes her. I can tell."

Dan forced himself to unclench his hands and moved them onto his lap beneath table height. "I suppose so. I'm just responsible for her that's all. And I love her."

Jeremy laughed out loud. "Gnat's ass stretched over a barrel! I like that. Sounds cool."

Dan gave his son a condescending stare. Jeremy caught the hint and was silently reminded not to swear. "I mean … gnat's butt stretched over a barrel." He hesitated a moment. "Doesn't sound quite as cool though."

Joe Leif sat there quietly listening to the exchange. He had the luxury of understanding everyone's perspective. He could relate to Dan's protective feelings towards his wife, Donny's carefree attitude, as well as the unsophisticated feelings of a young boy soon to be a man. It was a talent he'd developed over all his years in dealing with people as a cop.

At that moment the outside door opened and General Branch stepped inside the house. Dan Branch jumped to his feet and snapped to attention. "Officer on deck!" As a reflex action, Donny Brewster snapped up to attention as well. Jeremy, who thought it was cool, jumped up and saluted. Donny Brewster cringed inside. He was going to have to teach the boy the proper protocol for when to salute.

General Branch stopped at the door and looked around the room as if on an inspection tour. Finally he nodded to Jackie who had followed in behind him. "Very good." She smiled. The old man walked over and sat down at the table. "Will you boys please sit down and relax. I've done enough saluting for one day. I just want to relax in the comfort of my own home for a little while."

The three men sat down. Joe Leif just crossed his arms and smiled. Rodney saw the look on his face and smiled back at him. "You must get a real kick out of all this, eh Sheriff?" The sheriff's grin broke out onto his face as he nodded.

"Do you remember the day I caught you stealing those solar panels, Rodney? Must've been just a few weeks after The Day."

Uncle Rodney nodded and the sheriff continued.

"You were still a chain smoker back then, and I was the sheriff and thought I was in charge. I gave you a lecture on stealing public property. And now look at you. You're the general of the whole darn world!"

Rodney looked him in the eye for a moment and then turned his gaze off into space as if imagining something no one else could see.

"Joe, there's a part of me that misses those days, the days of peace, the days of calm, the days of preparation for something greater and something turbulent." He chuckled and returned his gaze back to Joe's face. "But it's just a small part of me and getting smaller every day. We have so little time for reflection these days, but the time to reflect isn't during the heat of battle, but after the smoke has settled, after the blood has seeped back into the ground, after the war is done." He hesitated. "And once again ... the heat of battle is upon us."

All three men and one boy looked Rodney in the face. He had their attention.

"Gentlemen ... there is a new threat."

CHAPTER 11

"**P**RESENTLY, WE ESTIMATE THEIR strength to be just over twenty-five thousand men along with several thousand women who render logistical support. Unlike The Horde, they are well supplied with military transport vehicles, such as Humvees, even some Heavy Expanded Mobility Tactical Trucks. They possess a large assortment of light and medium military tactical vehicles such as the M1126 Stryker armored fighting vehicles, along with Bradley fighting vehicles, which you are already familiar with. In addition to that they have access to F-18 fighter jets and an assortment of cargo and attack helicopters. They are here, just north of Grand Rapids in a small town named Rockford and heading north at the rate of ten miles per day."

Rodney Branch stood in the conference room of the old courthouse drawing on a chalkboard. Seated just a few feet away were Colonel Dan Branch, Sheriff Joe Leif, Sergeant Donny Brewster, Major Larry Jackson, Captain Ed Brown and Captain Danny Briel. Dan looked around the room and to the back. There was a man in civilian clothing sitting there whom he didn't know. His Uncle Rodney had shook his hand and spoken to him briefly before the meeting. He appeared to be in his mid-fifties, with graying blonde hair, cut short, and with eyes that could penetrate steel. His presence made Dan feel uneasy.

"At that rate, assuming they continue north up the US 131 corridor, they will reach Kalkaska in fifteen days. Just as before, if they turn west toward Traverse City, we will be in their direct path."

General Branch paused and looked around the room. "Are there any questions?"

At first, no one spoke. Sheriff Leif was surprised at the silence and even more surprised when he heard himself speaking.

"So how many Marine Corps snipers will it take to kill them all?"

The general smiled slightly. "More than we have." Joe Leif nodded his head but didn't follow up with another question. Dan Branch was the next to speak. "Why is everyone coming up here into the middle of nowhere? It doesn't make any sense. There's nothing up here but trees and cold weather most of the year. Why aren't they going south to the big cities and better climate?"

General Branch didn't answer right away. He had that thoughtful, contemplative look on his face like he always did when deciding how much to say of what he really knew. He looked around the room, making eye contact with each person one at a time. Finally, he spoke in one terse sentence.

"It's me ... they're coming after me."

There was silence in the room. Dan's brow furled. Joe Leif looked over at him, and Dan glanced back. Everyone seemed confused, but Joe was the first one to put the confusion into words.

"Listen, Rodney, I'm just a country cop who doesn't know much about global warfare, so I don't understand a lot of things that are going on right now. But I'm no idiot either. Will you please explain to all of us why twenty-five-thousand Islamic warriors are going two hundred miles out of their way to kill one man?"

Uncle Rodney didn't answer. He just stood there in front of them, not quite sure what to say. The sight of it made Dan sad. He'd never seen his uncle this way before. General Branch bowed his head, but didn't speak.

"General Branch, I'd like to answer that question if you don't mind." The stranger in the back stood to his feet and strode up to stand beside Uncle Rodney. The general smiled weakly, then squeezed the man's right shoulder before turning back to the room.

"Allow me to introduce Special Agent Jeff Arnett of the Central Intelligence Agency."

General Branch sat down in the front row and placed his hands on his thighs while the man readied himself to talk. Jeff Arnett was a tall man with a hawkish nose that dominated his face. He appeared to be around fifty-five years old with short hair, once blonde but now mostly gray. The man spread his feet shoulder width apart, square to his audience. Donny Brewster and General Branch seemed to be the only men in the room not intimidated by this new stranger.

"General Branch is correct. I am with the CIA, or, more correctly, I *was* with the CIA back before The Day. Shortly after the terrorist attack on the power grid, all elements of the federal government fell into disarray, and the CIA was not immune to this. One man came forth and offered each CIA agent an opportunity to be a part of the new government which he was already forming. He'd been planning it for years, and this one man, Jared Thompson, AKA The Blind Man, had amassed an ill-gotten fortune with which to buy loyalty and solidify logistics in preparation for the collapse. The CIA and FBI had been studying Thompson for years, trying to build a case against him, but he never did anything against the USA and operated mostly outside the country. So we left him alone for the most part. I realize now that was a mistake.

"I am one of the few people left alive to have had the opportunity to personally meet Mr. Thompson. Most people who see him in person happen upon mysterious deaths shortly thereafter. I was an exception because, quite frankly, he screwed up. He misjudged me, assuming I would join his cause. That is one of his flaws: he assumes that all people act selfishly, out of loyalty to themselves and no other, that every man has a price, and when offered that price, they will sell their very souls to achieve power and pleasure."

He looked down at the white tile floor, and paused for a moment before going on. "To be honest, I have to admit that I was tempted. I knew the world was going to hell in a hand basket, and was not likely to revive in my lifetime. I have no family to hold me accountable, so … yes, I was sorely tempted."

He looked back up. "But, instead, I contacted Colonel MacPherson of the Shadow Militia and, after being thoroughly vetted," He turned to Rodney and smiled briefly "Vetted with extreme prejudice I might add … I met with General Branch. Homeland security had been following the rumors of an underground militia for some time, but all leads came up empty. My contact with Colonel MacPherson was a last-chance shot in the dark which paid off.

"I am now a proud member of the Shadow Militia and work very hard to head up their clandestine intelligence service. I am qualified to do this based on twenty years in the field as an operative. My last ten years have been spent as a mid-level supervisor with an intelligence analyst group.

"And now, Sheriff Leif, with that background info out of the way, I'll answer your question." He looked Joe square in the face. "In the eyes of The Blind Man, General Branch and The Shadow Militia are public enemy number one. He believes them to be the greatest obstacle standing in his way of ruling North America." His gaze moved from Joe to General Branch before continuing. "And he is correct in that summation. There is no one person or organization on the entire planet better equipped to halt the evil now descending on

America and then the entire world." He halted abruptly, took a deep breath and then continued on. "You see, Rodney Branch and the Shadow Militia are anathema to The Blind Man, simply because he cannot and will not ever understand them. In that one sense he truly is blind. He is blind to anyone with enough honor and integrity to sacrifice and die for his fellow man. And therein lies his major weakness. In order to *defeat* your enemy, you must *know* your enemy. And he can never truly know a man of honor. His only chance of victory is to corrupt enough pure hearts to overcome the Shadow Militia. He must erase all vestiges of hope and light from the land.

"But before he can do that he must first destroy the Shadow Militia. But the Shadow Militia cannot be destroyed without first killing this person you all call Uncle Rodney. You see, the Shadow Militia isn't just an army; it's a hope; it's a beacon of light, shining in the darkness for all to see. It gives all people everywhere a clear choice between good and evil. And Jared Thompson must eradicate that choice."

There was silence in the room.

No one moved. No one scratched their head or shifted nervously in their chairs. To any onlookers, they could have been mistaken for storefront mannequins on display.

Finally, Major Larry Jackson stood resolutely. "I say ... we get ready to kick this Blind Man's ass clean on back to whatever rock he crawled out from under!"

Captain Briel stood beside him. "I'm with Larry. I say we kick his ass!"

Dan Branch and Donny Brewster both stood in unison and simply nodded to the general before coming to attention and saluting. Captain Brown stood to attention and saluted as well. Soon every person was on his feet, saluting General Branch.

Except for one man.

Sheriff Joe Leif shifted nervously in his chair. "What the hell have you gotten us into this time, Rodney? You are such a pain in the ass! I can understand why The Blind Man wants to kill you. You …" He let the words go un-uttered. Joe let out a huge sigh before slowly standing to his feet, like an old man doing work he once found easy, but was now beyond his years and his ability. Sheriff Leif snapped to attention and saluted Rodney Branch.

The old general doggedly moved to his feet, humbled by the show of fealty. Rodney stepped to the front of the room, faced them all and gave them his best Marine Corps salute. He held it for a full five seconds. Then he snapped his right arm down and said, "Please be seated."

Special Agent Jeff Arnett returned to the back of the room while the others sat back down. There were a few excited murmurs, but Rodney shushed them with a raise of his hand.

"I thank you for your commitment, but, quite frankly, that was the easy part. You have all proven yourselves in battle, proven to be worthy of my trust, my devotion and my very life. For that I thank you."

He stepped over to the chalk board, picked up the red rag beside it and wiped away the writing.

"I have a plan. It will take a lot of work and a lot of sacrifice. Many of us will die, but, if it works … it will leave the world with hope."

Sheriff Leif bowed his head and chuckled out loud. "Hell, Rodney. Sacrifice, hard work, lots of us dying … sounds like the same plan you had last time. What's not to love?"

In the back of the room, Special Agent Jeff Arnett smiled. He liked this group already.

CHAPTER 12

June 27th, A Spy is Born

UNCLE RODNEY STOOD JUST INSIDE the pole barn door with one shoulder propped against the door frame. This was Harold Steffen's old home, and Jeff Arnett was now setting up a computer network inside the very pole barn where Harold and Jackie had repaired the old crop duster used to save Iroquois from The Horde. Rodney had set up the location himself, citing its remoteness. On the outside it would continue to appear abandoned, but, on the inside, it would be a modern, pre-The-Day computer intelligence analysis center.

"Why do you want to do this, Jackie? Answer all my questions in Arabic, please."

The voice was that of Special Agent Jeff Arnett. He was standing before Jackie Branch, wearing blue jeans and a black t-shirt. She responded quickly in fluent Arabic.

"I don't want to do this. Only a crazy person would want to do this."

Jeff responded immediately.

"Then why are you doing it?"

"Because I want to help my family. I want to fight the evil that is coming to us. And because I appear to be the only one who can get the job done."

Jeff nodded.

"But aren't you afraid?"

Jackie smirked at him.

"Of course I'm afraid, you idiot! But no more afraid than my husband when he goes into battle and people are shooting at him."

Jeff folded his arms across his chest before going on.

"What is your biggest fear?"

"My biggest fear is that I fail and dishonor my family."

Jeff cocked his head to one side.

"Are you not afraid of dying?"

Her response was immediate.

"Of course not! I'm a Christian! To live is Christ and to die is gain."

"You really believe that?"

Jackie snapped back at him.

"Cut the foolishness and get to the heart of your testing! I don't have time for this. I want to get this done and get back to raising my family!"

Jeff looked over at Uncle Rodney and smiled.

"She's a feisty one."

Rodney nodded.

"I told you. She's a Branch through and through. She can do it."

"But Rodney, you don't understand. Her feistiness could get her killed. She's moving into a barbaric, male-dominated society and any hint of dominance could get her tortured and … well, tortured and many other unspeakable things. She speaks the language perfectly, like a native almost. She knows the culture, the religion, even how to cook the food, but, hey, let's face it, subservience is not her strong point, and Islam is all about submission."

Just then Jackie fell to her knees in tears. Her weeping appeared sincere as real tears fell from her eyes and onto her cheeks. She clutched desperately at Jeff's trouser leg and bowed her head low to the ground as she spoke.

"Please, master, please give me a chance to serve the

Supreme General in the cause of Allah. Just give me some small token job to serve and support the warriors of Jihad!"

At first, Jeff Arnett looked surprised, then his face broke into a smile. "Now hey. That was good. Really good. You could have been a field agent in the CIA."

Jackie reverted back to English and to her cocky manner. She stood proudly to her feet and threw her shoulders back and raised her head. "I never trusted the CIA. But I can be a field agent for the Shadow Militia."

She looked over at Rodney, who was beaming proudly at her like a father watching his daughter at the altar.

"We have a few more details to work out. Then, right after Dan leaves for combat, I'll insert you into the Islamist army so you can strike a blow for freedom."

Jackie lowered her head. "I don't feel right about doing this behind Dan's back."

Rodney moved forward and put his right arm around her shoulder. "I know, Jackie. And I don't like it either. Normally I wouldn't do it. But ... I just don't see an alternative. This is a chance to save thousands of lives and ..."

Jackie interrupted him. "I know. And the needs of the many outweigh the needs of the few."

Jeff Arnett laughed out loud. "Oh my god, she's quoting Spock! She speaks fluent Arabic, is a fantastic actor, and on top of all that she's a Trekkie!"

Jackie nodded and raised her right hand into the air in front of her. She separated her ring finger from her middle finger in a perfect Vulcan salute.

"Live long and prosper."

General Branch tried to laugh with them, but the emotion wouldn't come. He was sending his loved one, the wife of his adopted son into almost-certain death. If it didn't go well ... He let the thought slip away, cordoning it off with all the other partitioned emotions inside him. It was hard being a general, but even harder to command the ones you loved.

Jackie saw the look of concern on his face, and reached out with her right hand, placing it on the old man's grizzled cheeks. "It's okay, Uncle Rodney. Do you remember what I said when we first met? You asked me who taught me my sense of honor."

Rodney nodded. "Yes, I remember. That was the moment I started respecting you."

Jackie let her hand drop back down. " I developed my sense of honor after six months in the wilderness watching Dan and Jeremy risk their lives and shed their blood and sweat for the safety of my daughter, myself and my now-dead husband. We were strangers, but they took us in. They would have died for us. And now, if need be … I'll die for them."

Rodney lowered his head. Jeff Arnett tried to reassure him. "It's a good plan, General Branch. A damn good one. Just say the word and we go."

But Jackie answered first. "Of course we go! The issue was never in doubt. We are Shadow Militia. We are warriors, and this is the right thing to do so we do it no matter the risk or the cost!"

Rodney raised his head and smiled. He knew she was right. But it seemed the older he got the more difficult these decisions became, and the more he hated making them. He sighed and nodded resolutely.

"Yes, we go."

Off to Battle

COLONEL DAN BRANCH LOOKED OUT ACROSS THE NEAT formation of soldiers in front of him. To his left were several hundred of the Home Guard, most of them veterans of the last battle. To his right was the entirety of the newly formed and trained Iroquois Militia Rangers. They were five hundred strong and far superior in experience and training to the group he'd commanded in the last battle for Iroquois City. The Home Guard would be deployed to the South to await the Supreme

General's arrival. The Militia Rangers would continue on south to meet the Supreme General. It would be a hit-and-run strategy, similar to before, but this time they'd be engaging close to thirty thousand troops instead of three thousand. The Horde had been an angry rabble without air support, whereas Supreme General Abdul Al'Kalwi was highly disciplined and motivated. Dan gave extra weight to their enemies air support. He still recalled with pain and sadness the day his previous command had almost been wiped out by one helicopter with infrared capabilities. This time, he would not make that same mistake. If they were to be killed, the enemy would work for it and be forced to hunt them down and kill them one soldier at a time.

Colonel MacPherson had been impressed with Dan's strategy saying it was the right plan for the right time. His uncle, however, had said nothing, and that worried Dan. As Dan stood at attention, looking out over his troops, he couldn't help but think to himself, *They outnumber us thirty to one. How can we possibly prevail?* But he was careful never to voice his fears, even to his wife ... especially to his wife.

Jackie had been surprisingly supportive this morning when he'd left the house, and that worried him. Normally she would raise a fuss and try to talk him out of it, but her lack of resistance made him suspicious. He recalled the several times Uncle Rodney had sent her private messages via courier. The meetings she'd had with Special Agent Arnett also came to mind. Jackie and Uncle Rodney were up to something. But it would have to wait until he got back home ... if he got back home.

Major Jackson was beside him, flanked by Captain Briel. Captain Brown was heading up the detachment of Home Guard. Dan's own son, Jeremy, had left the night before with Sergeant Donny Brewster on special assignment with a unit of seventy-five snipers. Most of them were fully trained in the sniper's art, combat veterans of the last battle, but inexperienced in this new method of warfare. He expected that many would do well, while others would not. Dan thought of his own son and winced. There was something about Jeremy that made him nervous, almost afraid. Jeremy had already killed, but … still, somehow, he retained his youthful excitement and glorious vision of war. The boy thought himself to be ten feet tall and bullet proof. Donny had promised to take him under his wing and keep him protected, but that had been little comfort. Because Dan knew that if Jeremy was with Donny then he was sure to be in the thickest of the battle and therefore in extreme danger.

He pushed all these thoughts out of his mind for now. The time for reflection and regret would be days from now after the battle, and only if they were still alive. Dan watched as each Company Captain marched to the head of formation and posted in front of their unit and saluted. Colonel Branch returned the salute.

"Battalion! Parade rest!"

In unison, the boots of eight-hundred men moved to the right and slammed down on the hard-packed earth of the parade ground as their hands moved with precision behind their backs. If their enemy had been only three thousand of The Horde, he would have been impressed with more confidence, but that was not the case and he was not optimistic. He believed in his heart that most of them would die.

"We are about to embark on a mission of historical proportions." Dan paused. Why did that sound pompous and melodramatic to him. He started over, this time with less flare and with a colloquial tone of voice.

"Listen, men. Most of you have done this before. You're smart, so you know that some of us will die. All I can do is promise you I'll do my best to get as many of you home safely as I can. I'll make my best decisions. I'll push myself harder than I push you. I'll put my own life at risk as much as I risk the ones who serve under me. I'll ignore my fear and let my courage come to the forefront in battle. I won't surrender. I won't retreat. I will die alongside you if need be."

The men were all stone-cold silent as he spoke. "However, all of you know I have a wife and kids to protect as do most of you. And that's what we fight for. We fight for the ones we love, the ones too weak to fight for themselves. Duty, honor, sacrifice, they are more than just words. Because it's the shedding of our blood that give words meaning and purpose."

Dan hesitated. He saw Joe Leif and General Branch off in the distance to the west. They were listening silently. But what Dan didn't notice was the small drone circling overhead. It was small as a hawk, capturing his words and sending them back to his master a thousand or so miles away.

THE BLIND MAN PLAYED THE RECORDING OVER AND over again, hanging on every word Colonel Branch spoke. He was impressed and filled with a sense of awe and confusion. While he was awed at the man's eloquence and courage, he was equally confused by the man's misguidance. They were determined to fight him to the death over a silly word called freedom. In reality he didn't want to dominate them, only to lead them, guide them in rebuilding America. Jared didn't see himself as a despot or a killer, but as a regal king with a royal destiny to any who would pledge their loyalty to him. Instead of fighting against him to the death, they would be better served to join him and aid in the re-unification of America. Only then would he be able to restore some vestige of freedom to the land.

Jared shook his head from side to side nonsensically. They were all brave fools, and they would all have to die. What a waste of incredible courage. It made him angry.

"Mr. Thurmond!"

Sammy moved up to his side immediately.

"Get me everything we have on this man. His name, birthplace, age, family, everything. He's a danger to us, and if he squats down to defecate then I want to know about it."

Jared made a clicking sound with his lips and teeth. "Yes, what a waste ... a terrible waste."

Sammy nodded his head and left the room. A part of him couldn't help but admire the reckless abandon of a man fighting for his home. Sadly, he knew all men like Dan Branch would soon be dead.

CHAPTER 13

July 1st, The Big Slow-down

SUPREME GENERAL AL'KALWI looked on in sheer horror and rage as the man to his left exploded in a mist of red blood and white bone. It was as if the man's head had spontaneously disintegrated as he watched for no apparent reason. But Abdul knew the reason. It was the snipers. The Blind Man had warned him of this tactic, but he was amazed at its effectiveness. For the last three days the entire column of thirty-thousand strong marching down the US 131 corridor had ground to a crawl. Instead of ten miles a day, they were now lucky to make five.

The Apache helicopter was quick to react as it sped angrily over to the hilltop like a crazed hornet. The first day of the attack it had been easy to subdue the snipers. With the Apache's infrared and machine guns they'd quickly located the sniper and then blew him apart. But on the second day something changed. The sniper attacks were more coordinated. Instead of one rifle shot, there had been twenty, but all coming from different locations at the same time. The three Apache helicopters he had at his disposal were kept busy, but never seemed to make it to the target on time. Even with infrared capabilities, the snipers just seemed to vanish into thin air. He needed to know how they were doing it.

Abdul looked down at the body beside him. He'd forced the man to wear his own Muslim ceremonial garb as a test. Now he knew they were targeting him and this made it personal. He thought for a moment. He couldn't blame them. He could hate them, but not blame them. It's exactly what he would do in their position. In fact, this type of hit-and-run guerilla warfare is what his people and his ancestors had been doing for decades with great effectiveness. But The Blind Man had given him the name of his enemy, General Rodney T. Branch of the Shadow Militia. More importantly, he'd given Abdul the name of the town where the man lived: Iroquois City.

Even at their present rate of five miles per day they would reach Iroquois in thirty days. They were losing approximately one-hundred soldiers every day to snipers. Abdul quickly did the math. Thirty-thousand minus three-thousand is Twenty-seven thousand soldiers remaining. He smiled. Negligible. Not a factor. He thought to himself *You'll have to do better than that General Rodney T. Branch. Much better.*

The Supreme General raised his left forefinger and a man instantly moved to his side. "Give the command to all lieutenants, 'Shoot every man who takes cover from the snipers. Explain to them their chances of death by sniper fire are less than the surety of death at my hand should they flinch or feint in battle.'"

The man moved away and began to disseminate the order. Five hundred men died that day from friendly fire plus one-hundred by sniper fire. But an amazing thing happened. The next day instead of five miles, the Supreme General's army advanced twelve miles.

THE ALARM CLOCK WENT OFF AND JASON REACHED OVER and slammed the button on top. The incessant buzzing sound stopped as quickly as it had started. He rolled over to kiss his wife good morning, but she was already gone. In fact, the kids must be gone as well, because their upscale ranch house in the suburbs of Grand Rapids was uncharacteristically silent. The big man just lay there in bed for a moment soaking in all the peace. Then his day started to get busier as he was reminded of all the meetings he had, the accounts he had to balance, and the facts and figures and graphs he'd need to remember in order to make it through the day's work.

Starbuck's. He needed hot, black coffee, maybe a double-shot espresso with a double-fudge chocolate brownie for breakfast. He thought about getting up but knew as soon as his feet hit the floor the day would change, mutate and spin out of control at an unbelievably fast pace, and he wanted so much for it to stay slow, like this, just laying here all alone with no responsibility nor care in the world.

As he lay there thinking about it between the clean, flannel sheets, soaking in the warmth and comfort, rain began to fall into his eyes again. His eyes fluttered open reluctantly, and he felt the rain wash down his neck and run lengthwise between his camo shirt and the water-soaked skin of his back.

"Lieutenant Little! Lieutenant Little! Wake up sir."

His eyes popped open for good now and he saw his sergeant looking down on him. The sky above was clouded over but still some light filtered down to reach the wooded floor where he lay in a puddle of water and mud. Bracken ferns reached up around him, and their pungent aroma, mixed with black coffee reached his nostrils.

"Sir, the colonel has called a meeting for all officers. You meet in his HQ under the big oak in ten minutes, sir. Here's your coffee sir."

Jason Little sat up slowly and looked at the sergeant. He reached out for the coffee and was soon sipping the cold liquid. He remembered his dream and could almost feel the warmth of the flannel sheets, hear the silence of his beautiful home in Grand Rapids. It was burned to the ground now. His wife was dead, killed in the last battle for Iroquois City. Coffee grounds stuck in the spaces between his front teeth. But it was good and strong. It seemed to start his heart again and get him moving.

Jason took a few more sips and moved slowly to his feet.

He picked up his AR-15 and walked slowly over to the big oak tree. "Thank you sergeant. Make sure the men keep their feet dry and their guns cleaned and oiled."

Jason thought to himself *Clean guns and dry feet.* What a joke. They'd been marching almost nonstop for three days and most of them would probably die with waterlogged feet and rusty weapons. When he reached the oak tree he sat down on the ground again and sipped his cold coffee while waiting for the other officers to arrive.

COLONEL DAN BRANCH STOOD UNDER THE TREES FACing an array of twenty or so officers and staff noncoms. The rain had stopped, and the sun was now trying to peek out through the clouds overhead. Eventually it would win the battle, but not before the wet and cold men began to shiver. It had been an unusually cold night for July, even in northern Michigan. Most of the men sipped canteen cups full of cold coffee. Dan had given strict orders that no one should build a fire of any kind as they were within ten miles of the advancing enemy army of almost thirty thousand troops.

"Sergeant Brewster and his Snipers have been successful in slowing the enemy advance for the last three days, but his tactics are no longer working, so we have to try something different."

There were no chalkboards, no flip charts, no computer screens to help Dan with the presentation; it was just one man talking to his comrades out in the boonies.

"So now it's up to us. Of course, the snipers will continue to kill as many as they can, but, truth is, we have only sixty-five snipers remaining, and the numbers just don't add up. They could shoot nonstop for days and still not be able to halt the enemy advance."

Dan looked at them all like dead men. He knew their chances of success this time around were slim, but still ... they had to do their best, and just hope that Uncle Rodney had some plan up his sleeve.

"We're going to launch a coordinated attack on three fronts."

Jason Little's ears perked up. *Did the colonel just say five hundred men were going to attack thirty-thousand men?*

"All sixty-five snipers will begin shooting at exactly eighteen-hundred hours. They'll still have the setting sun at their backs and adequate light to make good shots. They'll be transitioning from head shots to groin shots from here on out.

"As soon as the attack commences we expect the enemy to engage their light armor in a counterattack as quickly as possible. In fact, we're counting on it.

"As soon as the snipers begin shooting, a second force led by me will attack from the east at a range of fifteen hundred yards. This will undoubtedly result in an air strike by the three Apache attack helicopters. Normally this would result in a complete massacre of our troops as the Apaches have enough firepower with their M230 30-millimeter chain guns to kill us to the last man, however, we have a surprise for them, courtesy of General Branch."

Lieutenant Little smiled to himself thinking, *Okay, that's good, we won't be killed instantly then.* Jason quickly did the math in his head and raised his hand. Colonel Branch looked at him with an annoyed stare.

"Yes, Lieutenant?"

"Well, Colonel, I'm no accountant, well leastwise not any-more, but I just did the math and in order to win this battle each of us will have to kill sixty men."

Dan sighed to himself before answering. "No, lieutenant, not really. The mission isn't to kill all the enemy; our goal is to slow them down."

Jason Little squirmed in the mud, not really wanting to point out the obvious. "But, sir, and I mean no disrespect by this, but … if the enemy attacks with their light armor, and, we have no way to stop them, then … aren't we all going to die?"

Dan Branch couldn't help but smile. Jason Little was a smart-ass and a pain in the butt, nonetheless, he liked him.

"It would seem that way, lieutenant. However, if you'll allow me to finish detailing the plan, I think we might be able to give you all at least a moderate chance of survival."

Jason smiled. "Oh, by all means continue then. I'm all ears."

Dan nodded and outlined the plan in detail. Afterwards, he dismissed the men. In four hours they would launch … and, live or die.

CHAPTER 14

In Dire Need of Hope

AT HIS HEADQUARTERS BACK IN Escanaba, General Branch and Colonel MacPherson waited for reports to come in from the battle south of Big Rapids, Michigan. It would begin at any moment, and it affected him on a personal as well as a professional level. Dan was leading the attack, and his nephew, Jeremy, was now fighting in the sniper unit. Rodney understood the dangers of battle, of facing overwhelming odds, and he knew within a few hours both the men he loved could be dead.

"They'll be okay, Rodney."

General Branch turned around to look his friend in the eyes. Mac knew him too well. He always seemed to read his mind, even when he didn't want him to. "Maybe. It's a good plan, but … you know … things can go wrong, and nothing in war is a sure thing."

Mac nodded. "I know. But it had to be done. We needed to buy some time in order to figure out a way to stop them."

"I know, Mac. Just doesn't make it any easier. They were making ten miles a day and this attack, if it succeeds, will cut that distance in half."

They were both seated in Colonel MacPherson's office, Rodney behind the desk, and Mac in a padded chair off to one side. Mac picked up his coffee cup and took a sip.

"You still haven't told me how you plan to kill thirty thousand screaming Islamists without using air power and other classified Militia Ranger assets."

Rodney Branch took a sip of his coffee. Ever since he'd quit smoking, his coffee intake had dramatically increased. Eventually, when coffee was no longer available, he'd be forced to find some other emotional crutch.

"I just love the way you beat around the bush, Mac."

The colonel smiled and waited, but his general remained silent. Mac respected that and waited patiently, quietly sipping his hot coffee as Rodney leaned back in his chair and thought.

After five minutes, Rodney still hadn't said anything, so Mac left it alone. He would tell him when he was darn good and ready and not a moment before. It had never been Mac's job to pester his superior, but rather to support him using any means necessary. His role in this venture had always been one of support and encouragement.

And then it hit him. *What if Rodney didn't have a plan? What if there was no way out of this?* Mac didn't voice his doubts. It wasn't his place to doubt, but to believe, even when things looked hopeless ... especially when things looked hopeless.

JEREMY BRANCH LAY IN THE DITCH WITH HIS HEAD FACing the enemy encampment, shrouded in his Ghillie suit. It was open terrain, giving him a clear nine-hundred-yard shot. For the past three days Jeremy had been killing man after man after man with little time to reflect on his actions. But now, as he lay in his hole waiting for the alarm on his wristwatch to signal the attack, he had a few minutes to analyze the rightness and wrongness of what he was doing.

Donny Brewster had taught him the danger of thinking too much and of thinking too little. In order to become the best sniper possible, he had to believe in what he was doing without reservation, because even the slightest emotional or mental conflict could translate into a missed shot, either through unsteady nerves or irregular breathing. He'd learned in his training that everything had to come together perfectly to make those long-distance shots on man-sized targets.

That's why today, he was relieved his targets had been changed from men to vehicles ... in particular, gasoline tankers. His job was to poke as many holes in the sides of as many fuel trucks as he possibly could in sixty seconds, then beat feet out to the rendezvous point.

He was shooting one of Donny's rifles, an M40A5 with an effective range of nine-hundred yards, but Jeremy had already made chest shots two hundred yards beyond that. Now, shooting at large tanker trucks, hitting them would be a breeze. Donny had warned him not to be overconfident. Don't take the shot for granted and aim at the whole truck. Pick out a small point on the tanker and put the round exactly there. Jeremy guessed he could get off six good shots before bugging out.

It was odd. He'd been trained by a Marine sniper in personal one-on-one sessions, but he still felt like sixteen-year-old Jeremy Branch from Menomonie, Wisconsin who was sneaking out of the house at night to screw the neighbor girl. Had that life been less than a year in the past? It had. Though his whole life had changed, and he'd killed dozens of men since then, he still felt like the same kid inside. He thought to himself *God help me, I still have acne and I'm blowing people's heads off with little remorse.* Deep down inside he wondered *Will there be a price to pay for this? I'm doing the right thing. Everyone tells me I am. But it just doesn't feel natural.*

He still could remember the first man he'd killed just a few months prior to save his dad back in northwest Wisconsin. His father had been hanging by a rope, helpless to defend himself, while the man below him was about to shoot. Jeremy had killed the man without flinching, blown a big hole in his chest and then watched while the man had bled out. With horror, he still remembered the dying man's last words, "You're … a … boy?" He still remembered the crimson red spray landing out onto the snow. Even though he knew in his heart of hearts that he'd done the right thing and saved his father's life because of it, he still felt remorse. He'd confided this with Donny and immediately regretted his candor. "A good sniper feels regret and remorse after the shot. "A great sniper, the most effective at the art, feels only recoil."

Jeremy both feared and hoped that he would remain just a "good" sniper. The alarm on his watch vibrated on his wrist and he hunkered down to settle in for his first shot.

COLONEL DAN BRANCH HEARD THE FIRST SNIPER SHOT, then another and another. Soon the little valley on the US 131 corridor was ringing out with dozens of shots. He pulled up his binoculars and watched as thousands of enemy soldiers scurried to their pre-arranged rally points in response to the attack. Donny Brewster's intel had told him this would happen, and much of the plan revolved around it.

Dan waited for just the right moment, then nodded to the two men kneeling on the ground a few feet in front of him. The Mark 19 grenade launcher opened up, spewing several hundred 40 millimeter grenades to just the right place in the center of the encampment. Two other Mark 19s started launching as well. In all eight-hundred of the small bombs were lobbed into the motor pool at the center of camp.

Suddenly, without warning, a huge series of explosions rocked the ground as tanker after tanker ignited and threw flames up and out, spreading all over camp.

Dan watched for a few seconds in awe at the fiery maelstrom below. The innate part of him that prodded all humans to chase fire trucks and ambulances beckoned him to stay and watch the fire and carnage, but he resisted the urge to gloat over his handiwork. Dan quickly ordered the three Mark 19 teams to pack up and move down the far side of the hill. Within seconds they were gone.

Major Larry Jackson stood on the opposite side of the highway from Dan Branch. His job was perhaps the toughest and most dangerous of the three. Larry had deployed his men well; all five of the three-man teams were hidden inside the edge of the woods, but with a clear view of the sky. Major Jackson watched in awe as the flames below boiled up inside the center of the enemy encampment. He said aloud to no one in particular "Burn you raghead bastards!" The black smoke was rising higher now and blowing off to the east, leaving him in the clear. *Good. They'll still be able to find me.*

As he stood atop the hill in plain view, Larry hefted one of the smoke grenades back and forth in his hands. When he saw the first Apache helicopter rise up above the trees a mile away he pulled the pin, threw the grenade a few yards downhill and let the red smoke rise up. He did the same thing with a second and third grenade. Then he waited.

"Saracen Leader, this is Scimitar One. I have red smoke five hundred yards west of your location. Please advise if these are friendly or hostile, over."

There was a moment of silence as the Apache attack helicopter circled over the Supreme Leader's encampment.

"Scimitar One, this is Saracen Leader. We have no friendlies in that region. Engage and destroy enemy. Please acknowledge receipt, over."

Scimitar One continued to gain altitude as it switched to its infrared sensors. Scimitar Two and Scimitar Three rose up above the trees and took up position behind and to the left and right of Scimitar One.

"Saracen Leader, this is Scimitar One, we have infrared on sixteen targets. Beginning our attack now."

The pilot looked through the Integrated Helmet and Display Sighting System which was already slaved to the aircraft's 30 mm automatic M230 Chain Gun. Wherever he looked with his helmet, the chain gun followed. He smiled when he saw a lone man standing out in the open. He thought to himself, *Not the sharpest tool in the shed.*

Larry Jackson stood resolutely and alone on the hillside, watching the three Apache gunships come closer. They looked close enough to him, and he wondered why his teams hadn't engaged. *Has something gone wrong?* His eyeballs began to sweat as the gunships got bigger and bigger.

For a moment he thought about running, but then realized the futility of the notion. You can't outrun a Hellfire Missile or an M230 Chain Gun. He would either win … or he would die. In a moment of brave defiance, Larry raised his arm and waved his middle finger at the lead Apache. If he was going to die, at least he'd do it with some courage and style.

A moment later the first Stinger missile rose up from the hillside and streaked toward the lead Apache. The explosion raced across the sky as debris and flames scattered across the hill. A split second later four more Stingers groped up into the sky and soon the remaining Apaches were burning as they fell to the ground in smoking ruin.

Larry held his middle finger salute several seconds longer before dropping his arm. His heart was racing wildly, and then he saw the bullets tear up the ground around him from the small-arms fire below. They were already coming for him. He ran for the cover of the trees, glancing over his shoulder at the burning camp and the smoking aircraft.

"I never had a doubt."

Larry jumped on his quad and drove away with his five-man teams close behind him.

Five hours later, Supreme General Al'Kalwi sat in the Bradley Fighting Vehicle he used as his mobile command post and ground his finger nails into his palms. His second in command sat before him, sweat pouring off his face, and it wasn't from the heat.

"We estimate seven thousand casualties, three thousand

dead with another four thousand moderately or severely wounded. Many soldiers are suffering from headaches, concussions, smoke inhalation, second and third degree burns as well as shrapnel wounds."

"They are suffering for Allah. They should welcome the pain and thank him for it."

Abdul's eyes turned to fire as his right hand moved to grasp the hilt of his scimitar. He wanted so much to kill this man. Why hadn't he been warned against grouping all his vehicles in the center of camp beside the gasoline tankers? They should have foreseen this attack. By clustering their vehicles they had prevented sabotage but also unwittingly provided the enemy the means with which to destroy them in one fell swoop. Abdul spoke with a shake in his voice.

"And our vehicles?"

His lieutenant didn't answer right away. His eyes darted first to the left and then to the right as if looking for a means of escape. He started with the good news first.

"Most of the Abrams tanks were spared, protected by their thick armor, but a few were near the tankers and are still too hot to touch. Most of the Bradleys are okay, but the Strykers had their tires burned off and we have only a few spares. Their antennas were destroyed, so communication is limited as well. Again, we have few spare parts to fix them. Fifty percent of the HEMTT eight-wheel-drive heavy duty trucks are destroyed, most of the rest suffered minor damage. The Humvees are almost a total loss."

The Supreme General stood up as best he could and exited the Bradley. His underling reluctantly followed him. Once outside, Abdul drew his scimitar and turned to face his lieutenant. The smells of burning flesh, diesel fuel and rubber made it hard to breathe. He looked around him at the carnage as blood threatened to squirt out his eyeballs.

With sword upraised, he asked his lieutenant a very important question. "How long until we can be moving again?"

The lieutenant swallowed ruggedly before answering. He moved his right hand up to wipe the sweat off his brow.

"Ten days, sir."

Abdul moved closer circling the man like a panther ready to attack.

"I'll ask you again. How long until we move out?"

The man reconsidered.

"Five days, sir."

"So, tell me, which hand would you like to keep … your left or your right?"

He considered running, but knew he'd never make it. So he lied.

"We can move out day after tomorrow sir. I'll send teams to scavenge the area for petrol and we can work through the night on repairing the damaged vehicles. There are many repair facilities in nearby Big Rapids."

Abdul finally smiled.

"You are a good man, a good servant of Mohammed, peace be upon him. You have until morning to report back to me with your progress."

He sheathed his scimitar and waved his finger in dismissal. The man bowed low to the ground as he backed away, never taking his eyes off the Supreme General.

Once the servant was gone, Abdul looked again at the devastation around him. He sighed to himself. There was something The Blind Man hadn't told him, perhaps many things. And someday he would kill the Blind Man, perhaps torture the infidel first. He was sure of it. These were not mere farmers and peasants as the Blind Man had said. This attack hadn't come from farmers. It had been brilliantly conceived and carried out with flawless military precision.

The Blind Man had told him that a retired general by the name of Rodney T Branch lived in northern Michigan and had gathered up a small army of locals numbering about one thousand, composed primarily of farmers, factory workers and merchants. For some reason he'd failed to mention the Stinger missiles and the grenade launchers, not exactly standard issue to Michigan farmers.

He needed to find out more about General Rodney T Branch and this Shadow Militia. And, as an afterthought, *I'm going to need more helicopters.*

CHAPTER 15

JACKIE BRANCH HAD BEEN INSERTED into the Saracen camp three days ago and was now working as a scullery maid. The insertion had been easy as she'd simply walked into camp pulling a load of zucchini, summer squash and green beans in a small hand cart. She claimed in perfect Arabic that she worked in the kitchen and had been immediately let through the lines into the camp. Once inside she found her way to one of the many kitchen tents and began to work.

Jeff Arnett's instructions had been simple and precise. Blend in. Be plain. Don't be noticed. Look, feel and sound like everyone else and your chances of survival will go up exponentially. And that's exactly what Jackie did. Above all else, she was very careful to never make eye contact.

Her biggest challenge had been avoiding the "sex patrols". That's what she called them, because they were so loosely defined, but very precise in their purpose. They were unofficial, but prevalent, especially at night just before dark. Most women tried to stay out of the way so as not to be chosen, but it wasn't unusual for men to simply walk into the women's quarters and drag a victim out by the hair. Because of that, Jackie slept outside in the dark, usually in the cover of bushes or trees.

Jackie had been amazed at the carnage wrought by her husband's attack of three days earlier. The men were still burying bodies outside the camp and trying to get many of the vehicles running again. Seeing the widespread death caused by Dan and his men had helped her to better understand what her husband had been going through and why he didn't want her to be involved with it. He loved her and was protecting her.

Her second morning there she'd witnessed a public execution and seen the Supreme General for the first time. In full view of the entire camp, atop a building, Abdul Al'Kalwi, dressed in white, ceremonial robes had raised his sword and lopped off the head of his second in command. Jackie couldn't help but wonder why Donny Brewster didn't simply shoot the Supreme General from fifteen-hundred yards away. She knew he was out there and that he was fully capable of making the shot. But ... for some reason unknown to her ... this was not done.

Every day she watched as the Iroquois snipers shot armed men as they walked to and fro around the camp. On the first day alone she saw seven men die. The camp was huge and spread out for almost a mile going both north and south. She couldn't help but wonder how many of those men were killed by her son. It made her both sad and proud to know that Jeremy was out there, putting his cross-hairs on the people around her and pressing the trigger. She wondered if, perhaps, it was possible for her to be accidentally killed by her own son as she wandered around the enemy camp.

The vastness of the camp only made it easier for her to go undetected as she gathered information and watched under cover of anonymity. It was on the evening of the second day that Jackie executed the first part of Uncle Rodney's plan.

"WHAT DO YOU MEAN PEOPLE ARE NOT WAKING UP? I don't understand you."

The new second-in-command lowered his head and repeated the news to Supreme General Al'Kalwi. "There are five -hundred dead this morning and another two thousand who are not waking up. Some are awake, but cannot move. The doctor says that something is causing a paralysis of the respiratory muscles. People can't breathe so they die."

The Supreme General cursed aloud. "Bring me the physician!"

His lieutenant bowed as he left the tent and returned just a few moments later with the doctor in tow. The doctor bowed and stood in front of the Supreme General with his head politely lowered.

"Tell me what is happening!"

The doctor nodded and launched into the clinical explanation. "The victims appear to have ingested some sort of toxin. It appears to be a coniin alkaloid, derived from ..."

"Toxin! You mean poison?"

"Yes, Supreme General."

"How did this happen?"

The doctor lowered his head further as he explained. "Through multiple patient interviews I've come to believe all the victims had been drinking the night before. Those who reportedly drank the most are already dead. Others who ..."

"How is that possible?" He kicked the chair he'd been sitting in over to one side and swore again. "The great prophet, Mohammed, peace be upon him, forbids us to consume alcohol!"

No one in the tent was naive enough to believe alcohol was not consumed in camp. In fact, even the Supreme General knew it was common practice, and he condoned it by turning a blind eye. Unofficially, there was a three-hundred gallon tank of wine transported on the back of a large pick-up truck, and, as they went from town to town, scavenging, anyone who found alcohol brought it to the tanker and dumped it in. In times when alcohol couldn't be found, the men in charge of the truck made their own. The doctor continued by holding up a small leaf and some waterlogged seeds.

"These were found inside the wine tank. They are from the

plant called Conium maculatum."

Abdul was losing his patience with the man's medical gibberish. "Stop talking like a kafir and tell me what that is!"

The doctor lowered his head even further until his chin touched his pudgy chest. "It is from the poison Hemlock plant, sir."

Abdul turned to one side and stroked his beard, heavy in thought. He didn't understand what was going on. Everything had been so simple while attacking west. Jackson, Kalamazoo, Grand Rapids, even Lansing the State Capitol had been easy conquests, but ever since turning north ... Abdul was about to draw his sword and hack off the head of his new lieutenant, but something stopped him.

Ever since turning north ... It was the Shadow Militia!

He turned quickly to his lieutenant. "Ahmed! Get that Satellite phone we received from the blind infidel. We are talking to him immediately!"

And then as an afterthought. "The soldiers need to know what is going on. Proclaim to them that Allah is unhappy with their drinking and has passed judgment on those who disobey his laws and the edicts of the Supreme General. Anyone who continues to drink will be put to death. The laws of the Koran must be followed."

Ahmed scurried away to carry out his master's errands.

Sᴀᴍᴍʏ Tʜᴜʀᴍᴏɴᴅ sᴛᴇᴘᴘᴇᴅ ᴏᴜᴛ ᴏғ ᴛʜᴇ ʜᴇʟɪᴄᴏᴘᴛᴇʀ and walked toward the Supreme General. Sammy knew there were several reasons why The Blind Man had not come himself to the camp. One, his boss wanted to send a message that he was displeased with the Supreme General. Two, he wanted to establish a hierarchy where he was on top. And if he came when summoned .... he would appear to be a servant instead of the master. Three, and most important, the Shadow Militia had nukes, and he had to assume the Saracen camp was being watched. One radio call and The Blind Man would be glowing in the dark for the next five hundred years. So he'd sent

Sammy, his trusted servant. Sammy wasn't sure how he felt about that.

The F-18 fighters circled overhead running Combat Air Patrol while Apache gunships set up around the perimeter of the camp. Sammy was flanked by four men with MP5 submachine guns in full body armor and tactical vests. Another Apache hovered overhead with its chain gun pointed at The Supreme General's tent, which, of course, was designed to make him feel a little less supreme.

When Sammy met Ahmed, The Supreme General's second in command in the middle of the field beside US 131, he smiled to himself. Sometimes he felt like he was on the playground again, surrounded by testosterone and ego.

"Where is your boss?"

The second in command responded as forcefully as he could. "The Supreme General awaits in his quarters for your arrival. Where is The Blind Man?"

Sammy looked around the encampment. They'd been watching the past six days or so. The Shadow Militia's attack on the camp had been incredible. Secretly, Sammy had watched in awe and respect at the precision and creativity of the attack. He was enjoying the ringside seat. But his boss was concerned, as well he should be, about the incompetence of The Supreme General. He was fine against peasants when he outnumbered them a hundred to one, but then, who wouldn't be. The Blind Man had quickly realized that Abdul would need extra help if he was going to prevail or, at least weaken, the Shadow Militia.

"The Blind Man is watching the submarine races."

Ahmed's brow furled. His English was good, but it wasn't perfect. He didn't understand how The Blind Man could be watching a submarine race when he lacked eyesight. He also had never heard of the sport of submarine racing, and assumed it to be exclusive to affluent America. Or, perhaps it was just one of those idiomatic expressions the English language was prone to and made no sense at all. He hated the language.

"I see. I hope his submarine wins."

Sammy smiled and nodded. "Please, Ahmed, take me to your leader."

As Ahmed led him to the large, grandiose tent, near the center of camp, he wondered to himself *How did the infidel know my name?* Of course, Sammy knew everything about him as he'd studied his file before leaving on the mission. He was aware of the man's four wives and twenty-two children; that he had been born in Yemen before moving to America back in ninety-seven. Sammy knew the man cheated on his four wives often and that he enjoyed cocaine while he cheated. He even had photos.

"Supreme General, the Blind Man's assistant has arrived to answer your call, sir."

Abdul had been standing with his back to the door on purpose. Indeed, he'd even heard them enter, but refused to acknowledge them right away in order to establish his self-importance. Sammy's guards remained outside the tent alongside those of the Supreme Guard.

Abdul raised his right hand moved his four fingers in a dismissive fashion. Ahmed immediately bowed and backed out of the room. The Supreme General turned to Sammy Thurmond. Clearly, he was not pleased.

"Where is The Blind Man?"

Sammy replied with zero hesitation. His voice had lowered to his foreboding Hannibal Lecter decibel, and it sent a chill down Abdul's spine.

"He's watching the submarine races."

The Supreme General frowned and turned his back on Sammy Thurmond.

"I will speak with The Blind Man only after he apologizes for this insult. Now, it is time for you ..."

But Abdul's voice silenced when he felt the blade of Sammy's knife touch his throat. He reached slowly down to grasp his scimitar sword, but was surprised to feel Sammy's hand already there.

"Listen you ragheaded pig fucker. One move and I slit your worthless throat."

The Supreme General decided not to move.

"As a general you're anything but supreme. We've been watching you get your ass kicked by a bunch of farmers for the past week, and The Blind Man is losing confidence in your ability to conquer and rule Michigan."

Abdul's fear was turning to anger, but he dare not show it. "They are not farmers. They are experts in warfare and you chose to hide that fact from us."

"That's only because we know how cowardly you are, and we didn't want you to soil your holy robes and cry like a baby when you found out how worthy an adversary the Shadow Militia really is. Let's face it, Abdul, you don't even belong on the same battlefield with Rodney Branch. But my boss thinks you might be useful and could possibly even beat him, given the proper assistance. So here's what's going to happen."

Sammy pressed his knife just hard enough to draw blood as he talked. "I'm going to leave a file folder on that table over there and then walk away. You're going to read the contents of the file which contains everything you need to know and do in order to defeat General Branch. My F-18s and Apaches will stay in place over your encampment for the next hour. At the end of that time, if they've not seen a red flare go up over the camp, their orders are to attack and leave none alive. The red flare signifies your compliance with the contract. The contract simply states that if you destroy the Shadow Militia, then you will be allowed to live and rule all of Michigan. If you do not, then, well, then you will die a heinous death along with your entire army. Of course, your corpse will be given a proper burial in a nearby pig farm."

Abdul felt the knife move away from his throat. He pondered the deal for a moment. He could cry out and Sammy

Thurmond and his men would be killed, but not before Sammy killed him. Then the F-18s would attack and all his power and army would be gone. All his work would be wasted.

"I need more air support. My Apaches have been shot down."

The Supreme General slowly turned to find himself alone in the tent. Sammy Thurmond, the man with Hannibal Lecter's voice ... was gone.

Abdul's legs became weak and he collapsed on the grass of his tent floor. He felt the blood on his throat and tried not to cry. A few minutes later he struggled to his feet and moved to the table and the file folder. He opened and read. A smile came to his face. Perhaps ... this arrangement could work.

"Ahmed! Get in here!"

Five minutes later a red flare arced up over the camp and The Blind Man's air force flew away.

CHAPTER 16

An Evil Trap

J ACKIE WAS SURPRISED AT HER SUD-
den nausea as she spewed out the contents of her
meager breakfast onto the grass behind the kitchen
tent. Perhaps she'd contracted the flu or … maybe … perhaps
she could have been exposed to the contents of the deadly
plastic vial she carried in her pocket. But that didn't make
sense. The doctor had inoculated her against it. She should
be okay.

After wiping off her mouth and spitting several times on
the grass, Jackie reached into her pocket and grasped the
vial. This was her last mission, then she could head back to
Iroquois and her daughter. The past five days had not been
as glorious as she'd anticipated. Eating scraps, sleeping very
little, always paranoid and on full alert had left her physically
and emotionally exhausted.

Jackie moved around to the front of the tent where the large
pot of stew simmered over an open fire on a tripod. Conditions
in camp were a mix of twenty-first century technology and
medieval culture. Five times a day the call to prayer sounded
over loudspeakers, and, at the same time, people hauled water
from the stream to the west and boiled it for drinking. The
land had already been stripped nearly clean by The Horde and
other looters, so provisions were scarce.

She waited until the woman turned away to get something,

then she boldly walked up and poured the contents of the vial into the pot. Without stopping she quickly moved away from the tent and headed for the perimeter of the camp. She didn't want to be here when things started happening.

Escanaba HQ

JEFF ARNETT SAT ACROSS THE DESK FROM COLONEL MacPherson and General Branch, briefing them on Jackie's progress.

"The message received last night said phase one had been completed successfully resulting in an estimated two thousand enemy deaths."

Rodney Branch nodded his head in approval. "I told you she was tough."

Special Agent Arnett continued his briefing. "This morning we received word she had initiated phase two."

Mac was the first to respond. "How long until we know whether or not it's going to work?"

Jeff leaned back in his chair, annoyed by its lack of comfort. "The doctor says this is an enhanced version of Typhoid and should spread quickly. It's not likely to kill more than half of the enemy, but it will certainly take out anyone already weakened by the journey along with the sick, old and …" He hesitated. "The extremely young."

Rodney knew what that meant, and it was the reason he'd balked at employing biological warfare against the Saracen army. But, in the end, he'd relented to Mac's plan. Tactically it was sound and it was the right military response. For centuries collateral damage had always been exacted on the civilian populations. There was no way around it. And, in reality, it didn't matter what type of attack he made on the enemy, some civilians were guaranteed to die. War was dirty and not for the faint of heart. In the end … wars were only won by breaking things and killing people. Both Rodney and Mac understood that, however difficult it was now to carry out the plan. The important thing was this: it would give them more time to figure out a way to stop the Saracen tide from thoroughly overwhelming the state of Michigan.

"When will she be safely out of there?"

Jeff smiled. He'd grown fond of his pretty young pro-tege over the days he'd spent training her for this mission. "She should be out by nightfall. Then she'll rendezvous with Colonel Branch and his Militia Rangers."

Rodney smiled. He knew Dan would be furious at him for putting her in danger, but those personal elements would have to take a back seat to the greater good. If Jackie could kill another ten-thousand enemy troops, then he'd have a fighting chance of stopping them. If not …

"I'm sure the colonel will be both surprised and pleased to see his bride so soon."

Jeff shook his head. "You sure you shouldn't let him know what's going on?"

Rodney pondered his question for a moment. "Yes, I'm sure. Dan can be a bit passionate at times. I don't want the knowledge to affect his combat decisions. As far as it goes, he has no need to know the identity of his pick-up. Besides, he'll find out soon enough and all's well that ends well."

Jeff Arnett wasn't sure he agreed, but decided to let it go, at least for now. Besides, time would tell. "So, you said you have another mission to discuss."

General Branch nodded and stood up. He walked to the window and looked out at the Escanaba summer. It was beau-tiful in the warm months, but the Upper Peninsula winters froze him to his core, and the older he got the worse it affected him.

"Yes, but only you and I and Mac can know about it."

Jeff glanced over at Colonel MacPherson, then back at General Branch. "Well, lucky for you the CIA is very good at keeping secrets. What do you need?"

Rodney turned back around. "It's simple. I need you to

find out where I can get a freighter full of ammonium nitrate, 100,000 tons would be good. And I need to get it here within a week."

Special Agent Arnett cocked his head to one side. "Really? Just like that?"

Rodney nodded. "And I could use some nitromethane or maybe diesel or fuel oil if you can't find that."

Jeff smiled and shook his head from side to side. "What are you going to do ... blow up the whole Upper Peninsula?"

Rodney laughed softly. "No, not the whole peninsula, just selected regions of strategic importance." And then he added as an afterthought. "Besides, it's good stuff to have around, and I'm running low."

The tall man stood up and sighed. "Well, I can't tell you where things are right now, but I can find out where they were the day the lights went out."

"That'll have to do then. Just give me some options. It's important."

Jeff Arnett turned and walked out the door, closing it behind him. Ranger MacPherson looked over at his boss and stared. Rodney avoided his friend's gaze.

"So, did you come up with a plan?"

Rodney turned back to the window and watched the ducks on the overgrown lawn. They were pooping on everything, and it was driving him crazy. Back home in Iroquois he would have shot them or sent his dog, Moses, after them. He missed Moses.

"It's still half-baked, Mac. But it seems so desperate and terrible to me that I don't want to say it out loud quite yet. It needs to stew a while."

Colonel MacPherson didn't answer him. He knew from experience that it would do no good. When Rodney was ready to bring him into the plan, he would be there.

Spy Hunting

"THIS IS THE WOMAN WE ARE LOOKING FOR." THE Supreme General tossed the photograph onto the table and slid it over to his second in command. Ahmed picked it up and looked at it.

"She is Middle Eastern?"

Abdul nodded. "Yes, born in Lebanon. Then moved to America after her infidel father was killed by patriotic Muslims there. Her mother renounced the faith and turned to Christianity. The girl was raised in America and became a Christian missionary. She married the son of the Shadow Militia general, and now she is inside our camp as we speak. She is the reason our people are dying mysteriously. Catch her and bring her to me and you will be rewarded. Otherwise ..."

Abdul didn't finish the threat. There was no need as both understood the implications of failure.

"It will be done as you command Supreme General." Ahmed lowered his head and backed out of the room in holy submission.

The Supreme General looked down at the file folder in front of him. He wondered to himself ... *How had The Blind Man gotten all this information? He had to have been watching the Shadow Militia from the start.* He squirmed uncomfortably on the cushion beneath him. He thought to himself *It's not fair the infidels should have so much technology when the soldiers of Allah had little.* And then he heard a voice, or thought he heard a voice, whether it was coming from inside him or from without, he didn't know.

"The way of technology is the way of the kafir. But with you it is not so. The armies of Allah will succeed by virtue of strength and courage. You will triumph with the sword."

Abdul's smile spread across his face. He had just been visited by the great prophet, Mohammed, peace be upon him, and now all would be well. He was sure of it.

He placed his hand inside his robe and retrieved the plastic pill bottle. Inside was a fine, white powder which he spread onto the table in a line. Afterwards, he felt emboldened to carry out the will of Allah, confident he would win in battle, not just with General Branch, but also against The Blind Man and all his technology.

He stood to his feet and walked to the entrance of his tent. He moved the flap aside and looked out briefly up into the sky. Abdul wondered, *Can he see through the walls of my tent?*

IT WOULD BE DARK SOON, SO JACKIE HOVERED NEAR THE edge of the encampment. As soon as the last light began to fade, she would edge out into the darkness and be away from this God-forsaken place. She prayed quietly to herself for protection and for the night to come quickly. Her little girl must be missing her by now, and she wanted nothing more than to get back to her. Jackie vowed to herself, in the fading light as the campfires lit up one by one, *I will never do this again.*

A moment later there was a commotion from deep inside the camp. A part of her wanted to run, but she forced herself to be brave and patient, to stay with the plan. Running now would be suicide, and she knew her nerves were on edge. She just had to stay the course.

The camp seemed to come alive as more and more men picked up their arms in preparation of … something. She waited inside the protection of her grey-hooded cotton top. *Was the bioweapon already working? Were people already getting sick?* She didn't think it was supposed to work that quickly. But, if so, then it was all the more reason to get out of camp.

Finally, Jackie lost her nerve and began to walk out the perimeter of the encampment. Just as she was about to enter the field between the camp and the woods, a loud voice boomed out behind her.

"Stop!"

As a reflex action, Jackie froze in her tracks and turned her head slightly to see what was going on. Four men were looking directly at her and all were armed with rifles. In retrospect, she should have run, but hindsight was not available to her. The men moved toward her and soon she was in custody.

Just West of the Enemy Camp

THE LAST RAYS OF GOOD DAYLIGHT WERE FADING DOWN onto the horizon and in another thirty minutes it would be pitch black. Colonel Dan Branch lifted the binoculars to his eyes and peered down on the perimeter of the enemy encampment. The enemy camp hadn't moved since the last successful attack on the Saracen motor pool five days prior. They appeared to be focusing all their efforts on repairing as many vehicles as possible, an effort which Donny Brewster and his snipers had been exploiting as much as possible.

His orders had come directly from Uncle Rodney and they were very explicit that he should carry them out in person. He didn't understand it. A very important operative would be leaving the enemy camp at night fall. He was to meet him and take him back to safety where he would be extracted and flown back to Escanaba for debrief.

Dan assumed this person was a spy, and he wondered who it was and why he hadn't been told before now. He suspected this spy was somehow responsible for the mysterious deaths inside the camp which had been happening the past few days. Donny's snipers had been reporting more and more people being buried outside the camp to the east. If all went as planned, he'd be able to meet this man soon, and then he could hear the full story of what had been going on.

Whatever this spy had been doing, he just hoped it killed every last person inside that camp. There were still well over twenty-thousand enemy soldiers, and he knew in his heart there was no way the Shadow Militia could prevail against them. He suspected his Uncle Rodney knew that as well. Uncle Rodney would have a plan. He always had a plan.

Dan watched through his binoculars as the camp seemed to slowly come alive. Something was happening down there.

He glanced over at Captain Danny Briel beside him.

"You see that Danny?"

The captain beside him, who was also peering through binoculars grunted before answering. "Yup. Something's starting to happen down there."

Dan Branch lowered his binoculars for a moment to rest his eyes, but the captain's voice interrupted him.

"Colonel! Look at that!"

Dan raised his binoculars again and quickly focused in on a cluster of men at the edge of camp. Four guards had detained a person and were in the process of taping his hands behind him. Dan thought to himself *I hope that's not our spy.* Then he watched as the prisoner's hood was lowered, revealing the face of a terrified woman. Dan's heart skipped a beat as adrenaline surged into his bloodstream.

"Oh my God! No!" Colonel Branch started to get up, but Danny Briel quickly pulled him back down to the earth.

"What are you doing?"

"I have to get her!"

Danny shook his head.

"No way! Are you crazy?!"

Dan Branch looked into his captain's eyes with determination made of fire, but Danny Briel met his stare with ice cold of his own.

"If you go down there right now she dies and so do you. You need a plan of action."

Dan glanced at the enemy camp and then back at Captain Briel. His head knew he was right, but his heart wanted to attack with all the unbridled ferocity he could muster. And then it came to him. He recalled Jackie's meetings with Special Agent Jeff Arnett, the courier messages from Uncle Rodney to Jackie. They all made sense now. *She was the spy!*

Dan pulled up his binoculars and scanned the edge of camp, but his wife was already gone.

CHAPTER 17

July 4th, The Game Gets Tough

"**B**Y NOW YOU MUST KNOW THAT your spy, your daughter-in-law is in my custody. You must also know that life is very precarious, and that I can do anything I want with her."

The Supreme General hesitated before going on. He looked over at Jackie, who was duct-taped to a chair in the middle of his tent. She was naked, her body covered in dried blood and bruises. They had tortured her to get the code to unlock the satphone. Above all else, Abdul wanted to speak in person with the man who'd been driving him crazy for the past week. He wanted the man to suffer, and he wanted to listen as General Branch, once proud, cocky and confident, was reduced to groveling in his proper place as a kafir.

"She is naked now, in her natural state. A very attractive woman, even covered in blood. I need you to know how serious I am, so I'm going to rape her now while you listen. If you hang up before I finish, then I will cut her throat."

Uncle Rodney's blood began to boil inside him. He wanted to kill this man. Mac stood beside him in his office with a restraining hand on Rodney's shoulder. The colonel sensed Rodney's anger and moved his finger up to his lips in a hushing motion, then he took the satphone from his general. In an excited and desperate mock voice, Mac spewed out a frantic reply.

"No! Please no! You've proved your point! I know you are serious. Just please, don't hurt her anymore and you'll be given free passage all the way to the bridge."

There was silence on the other end and Mac continued. "I will call back my snipers and my militia units, and you will not be bothered again by us. Just … please, don't hurt my daughter."

Abdul smiled. He was still going to rape her, just not over the phone.

"Agreed. But, if you break your word she will die a slow and painful death." Abdul lowered the phone to end the conversation, but hesitated, then brought it back up to his ear. "Oh, and one more thing. My doctor has confirmed that the woman is pregnant. If you cross me, then two lives will end."

Jackie watched in terror as Abdul lowered the phone and pressed the button ending the call. A few moments later he moved up to her and signaled his men to lay her on the table with arms bound behind her and legs spread out.

And then, he broke his promise.

But, through it all, Jackie did not scream. She cleared her mind, then filled it with her most happy thoughts, images of her baby Donna, of Dan lying on the floor beside her, the two playing and laughing as she looked on in better times. In her heart she resolved herself to live. The good times would come again, but first … she had to survive.

Escanaba HQ

"WHERE IS THAT SON OF A BITCH!?" COLONEL BRANCH had just stepped off the Huey helicopter and was already walking past Colonel MacPherson. He neglected to salute and continued hurriedly into the colonel's ancestral home, which was now the temporary Shadow Militia headquarters.

Colonel MacPherson didn't try to stop him. He simply followed behind, letting the scene play out. It was all foreseeable. The guards at the entrance raised their carbines in salute as Dan rushed through the door and up the stairs to Mac's office. The office door opened with a crash as Dan raced in with both fists raised. He saw his uncle standing tall in his olive drab fatigues and headed straight for him swinging.

With his arms still behind his back in an "at ease" position, Uncle Rodney stepped to one side and let Dan's momentum carry him on by. The general took a step back and aimed and fired, hitting Dan squarely in the back. Dan's body jerked and spasmed as twenty-thousand volts of electricity coursed through his frame.

"It's good to see you, Dan."

Dan Branch lay on the desk face first, wanting to move, but unable to fight off the after-effects of the electricity. Rodney pressed the trigger again sending another jolt into his loved one. Dan swore and tried to get up, but collapsed onto the hardwood floor. Uncle Rodney pressed the trigger one more time and then moved around to sit at the chair beside the desk.

"Son, as soon as you're ready, I think we need to talk."

The Saracen Encampment

THE TWO MEN STOOD ON EITHER SIDE OF JACKIE AS THEY lashed her to the wooden cross with duct tape. Over her torso, she was wearing the tattered remains of her dirty t-shirt. Below her waist all she wore were the scant covering of her undergarment. First, her arms, then her waist, then her knees and ankles. By time they were done, she was affixed so securely they were able to hoist up the heavy cross and drop it down into the hole. There was a small wooden ledge for her feet, so she could stand on it and still bring in air to her lungs or else she would have suffocated.

When the cross hit the bottom of the hole her entire body shuddered at the sudden stop. But she felt no pain. She was beyond pain. Jackie didn't know how many times she'd been raped and beaten in the last twenty-four hours, but she did realize her body couldn't take a whole lot more. Oddly enough, despite the physical abuse, her mind was still clear and focused.

She tried to look around at the camp, but both her eyes were swollen nearly shut. The only thought in her mind was *Dan must be going crazy.* Jackie knew he must be close by, maybe even watching, because she'd been scheduled to rendezvous with him the night before outside the camp. She felt conflicted, wanting Dan to come in and rescue her, but also hoping he stayed away for his own safety. Jackie thought back to the first few months they'd shared together in that north woods cabin in Wisconsin. He was the bravest and most passionate man she'd ever known. She recalled their weird courtship, how he'd stood at the foot of her husband's grave and asked permission to marry her. What had seemed crazy then, seemed even more ludicrous now in retrospect.

But these were crazy times, so why shouldn't crazy things happen? Was crazy and bizarre the new normal? It appeared to be. How else could she have ended up duct taped to a cross in the midst of twenty-thousand Muslims? It was crazy, unthinkable, at least … in the old life before The Day. But now, almost anything bad could happen, and it usually did.

Jackie bowed her head and closed her eyes. She heard men jeering at her, but couldn't make out the words. She didn't want to.

The Blind Man

I ENJOYED READING YOUR REPORT, MR. THURMOND. You are always so precise and thorough. And I like your particular attention to detail. I find it refreshing in a time when so much anarchy threatens the world."

The Blind Man turned and paced slowly to one side, around the coffee table, to the wall, then back again. He bent down and picked up the crystal decanter and poured more brandy into his long-stemmed wine glass.

"But now I have more work for you, work that only you

can do, work I can entrust solely to you, my right-hand man."

Sammy Thurmond stood almost at position of attention before his master, listening intently, but without emotion. He didn't answer, only because no answer was required; therefore any reply would be considered by The Blind Man to be a waste of words.

"I find the Saracen encampment to be insufficient. The "Supreme" General is anything but supreme. He lacks creativity, military experience, and is ruled by his emotions. He's already lost a third of his force, and, at this rate, will not have adequate manpower to weaken General Branch, much less defeat him."

He took a sip of his brandy.

"I want you to return immediately with a large force of security specialists. The man isn't even capable of protecting his own perimeter much less defeating a real general on the field of battle. Do what you have to do. Use whatever resources are necessary, but make sure the little toy general makes it all the way to the field of battle in sufficient numbers to draw out the bulk of the Shadow Militia."

He turned and faced Sammy.

"I need General Branch to commit the bulk of his airpower and armor. I want the bulk of the Saracen army to reach Iroquois City. That is where the battle will be fought. He will protect his home town. That is his weakness."

Sammy Thurmond said nothing. He knew the one-sided conversation was over, so he nodded his head and left the room.

Donny Brewster Stands Watch

IT WAS A GRUESOME SIGHT TO SEE THROUGH THE HIGH-powered spotting scope, Jackie's body sagging in the heat of mid-afternoon sun. Donny noted the bruises, blood and the many swollen areas of her body. He doubted she would last much longer. Dan and Jeremy Branch had both been called back to HQ, and Donny guessed it was all about keeping him out of the area, so they wouldn't have to watch this. More importantly, so they wouldn't do anything rash that would get them killed.

Just then a ladder was placed against the cross, which was about twelve feet tall. A man climbed up with a cup and appeared to give her a drink of water. Jackie stirred momentarily, just long enough to take a few sips, before lapsing into unconsciousness again. Donny bowed his head down in despair. He had to figure out a way to get her back.

Just then, he heard the sound of fighter jets overhead, diving down toward the camp. The four F-18s pulled out of their dive and leveled off just in time to fly over the camp, leaving an army of terrorized Saracens in their wake. The man on the ladder fell off onto the ground.

Apache helicopters were coming in now, lots of them, so Donny packed up and headed further back away from the fringe of camp. With Apaches came infrared, and he was no match for that.

By THE END OF THE DAY, SAMMY THURMOND HAD EXerted complete control over all security aspects of the Saracen camp. He'd been careful only to insult The Supreme General privately, and then, just enough to force him into submission. Sammy knew that absent the overwhelming force of the Apaches and F-18s, Abdul Al'Kalwi would undoubtedly kill him in seconds. So Sammy was walking a fine line and he knew it.

Sammy didn't like change. It made him nervous. And he had noticed the change in his boss. The Blind Man was doing things he'd never done before, things like sending him into a camp of twenty-thousand people who wanted him dead. That was a big deal to him. Not that Sammy valued his life, or even had any aspirations toward retirement or any type of normal life. Normal had always bored him. Before, he'd never thought about the future; there was only the here and now, primarily because he'd enjoyed his job. It was exciting and it intrigued him. The Blind Man had intrigued him … but not so much anymore. For the first time since taking employment with Jared Thompson, Sammy Thurmond was beginning to wonder what his next step would be. And he knew that was a very dangerous place to visit.

Sammy watched as his men installed security cameras around the center of camp. They were high atop a portable tower and faced all four directions, and powerful enough to scan the entire camp and on into the woods. His own men had taken control of the perimeter, assuming command of hundreds of Saracens to bear the brunt of the grunt work. But make no mistake about it … Sammy Thurmond was in command.

Sammy looked over at the big wooden cross standing fifty yards to the east. He quickly barked out a command.

"I want her taken down and fed and exercised twice a day. She's no good to us dead." And then as an afterthought. "And no one is to hurt her. I want her strong and alert and obviously alive to the eyes of anyone watching."

Then he moved on to his new command post where he checked on the progress of launching the small drones. Sammy left nothing to chance when it came to security, especially his own security, and The Blind Man had rightly surmised that tying Sammy's fate to that of The Supreme General would be in his own best interest.

CHAPTER 18

DAN BRANCH WAS IN A HOLDING cell at the Delta county jail, sitting on a bench attached to the concrete wall. His wife was, at this moment, undoubtedly being tortured … or maybe she was already dead. But Dan couldn't think that way. He had to stay positive or he'd never get out of here and never be able to save her.

He stood up and paced to the opposite wall, then he paced back to the bench. He'd already done it a thousand times, but he couldn't bring himself to stop. For some reason Dan had always thought better while walking. As he paced back and forth, Dan envisioned himself sneaking into the enemy camp in the dead of night and rescuing Jackie. He would need intel, but he could do the rest on his own.

Suddenly, he stopped in mid-pace. *Does Jeremy know?* He had to. He was there, and he was a sniper with a high-powered rifle and telescopic sight. And what about Donny? Would he help him? He thought so. He wondered about baby Donna. Was she okay? Was she crying right now? Was she being taken care of? Dan had been led to believe that Jackie was taking care of the baby while he was out fighting, and that was the only thing that had kept him going, knowing that his family was safe as he put his own life on the line. He could fight with vehemence and tenacity, but only when he knew they were safe. His focus was gone now and he cursed his own emotions for distracting him. Back to the task at hand.

How will I save her? Dan resumed his pacing. Back and forth, back and forth, back and forth … like a caged tiger. He moved with deliberation and passion, thinking, plotting, planning.

"I KNOW WHAT THE PURELY MILITARY DECISION IS. BUT I don't like it."

Colonel MacPherson stood mutely beside his general, watching as Rodney stared off into the wall beside him as if it wasn't there.

"I know I should kill her or at the least let them kill her. I should renew the sniper attacks and continue rallying the forces to make our final defense. That's what I should be do-ing, not sitting here with you trying to figure out a way to save her."

Rodney stood up from the desk chair and began to walk back and forth in the office. Each time he reached the far wall he did a perfectly executed about-face and walked one-hundred-and-eighty degrees in the opposite direction. Mac watched in fascination at Rodney's incessant pacing, which seemed to be identical to that of Dan's. He knew the two men were linked together by some bond, something unseen, some magical bond of unseen blood. Suddenly, Rodney stopped his pacing.

"What do you think I should do, Mac?"

But the colonel didn't answer, and Rodney resumed the pacing as if he'd never stopped or even asked the question.

"What are the ramifications of killing her or letting the Saracens keep her prisoner?" He answered his own question. "Colonel Branch will become ineffective as a fighting leader. The Militia Rangers will have no one to lead them and they will be demoralized to the point of ineffectiveness as they are forced to stand by leaderless, watching the Saracen Tide ad-vance toward their homes and families."

He stopped pacing. "That is unacceptable." He paced again. "And if I mount a rescue attempt in a camp guarded by Apaches and F-18s, all who take part are likely to die and the rescue will probably fail. People will die in vain to save one woman."

The general looked over at Colonel MacPherson. "What am I missing, Mac?"

His friend shook his head from side to side. "You are seeing it clearly, General Branch."

Rodney resumed his pacing. The Shadow Militia had always been a lost cause. He knew that. In the old days, as a soldier for the United States military, he'd always had the upper hand, the advantage, the technology and superior numbers. But now ... the shoe was on the other foot and he hated it.

"I'm missing something, Mac. I have to be. There's always a solution. Every problem contains its own solution. I just have to figure it out."

Mac still didn't talk. He had no answers and no way to help his friend. Finally, in desperation, he threw out a suggestion. "Perhaps we could call upon God?"

Rodney halted and snapped to attention. He did a left-face and stared into Mac's eyes. Mac had never said that before. It must mean something. He brought his left hand up to his mouth and rubbed his face several times in deep thought. *What could it hurt?*

"Colonel MacPherson! Send for Father Connors. I want him here five minutes ago!"

Mac smiled slightly and walked out of the room while Rodney resumed his pacing.

The Saracen Camp

PEOPLE WERE DYING EVERY DAY BY THE HUNDREDS, AND the stench of the camp was quickly becoming more than Sammy Thurmond could bear. Already three thousand people had died from the mysterious sickness. Sammy had called The

Blind Man, who had immediately sent entire teams of doctors, scientists and medical personnel to protect his investment in the Saracen army. The doctors had quickly identified the sickness as a new strain of Typhoid, one not seen before.

Sammy couldn't help but frown when The Blind Man had cursed on the sat phone. He'd never heard him do that. Sammy Thurmond didn't like change; it was too precarious - too unpredictable, and he knew it was extremely hazardous to end up on the wrong side of change.

Already the weakest in the camp had died, but the doctors moved quickly to quarantine the sick and improve sanitary conditions. Sammy stood before the lead doctor now, questioning him on the prognosis.

"How many will die?"

"It's hard to say. No one can know for sure. We've never seen this strain before and it's quite hearty. Its high infectivity rate makes it difficult to contain. Fortunately, the lethality is only about forty percent."

Sammy Thurmond thought to himself. *Why do technical people talk like that, so fancy and formal?*

"How long until we can move again?"

The doctor seemed to be growing impatient. He wanted to get back to his work. He wanted to defeat this disease.

"These people can't be moved until they either die or until they beat the sickness. Sixty percent of them will live, but they'll need at least four weeks to recover and regain their strength. That's assuming the quarantine works and the sickness burns itself out. That's difficult because of the close quarters and the primitive living conditions here in the camp."

Sammy looked out across the camp at the hundreds of tents and vehicles. Three thousand had already died and another three thousand had taken sick. He knew The Blind Man would not accept a four week delay. He did the math in his head and quickly made a decision.

"Kill the three thousand sick as quickly and quietly as you

can. Anyone who comes down sick after that will be immediately shot. This sickness will end and it will end now. We move out as quickly as possible."

The doctor's lower jaw dropped open in disbelief. He turned to his colleague and said something in French that Sammy didn't understand. Then he turned back angrily.

"I will not kill anyone! I'm a healer, not a killer! And we will stay here and treat these people until every last one of them is well. We are doctors who've sworn a Hippocratic oath and …"

But his sentence was interrupted by the knife blade against his throat. The steel severed the windpipe and carotid artery leaving nothing but a gurgling sound and a spatter of blood. The red liquid hit Sammy in the cheek and he put away the knife slowly and pulled out a clean, white handkerchief. He wiped away the blood on his cheek and dropped the soiled cloth to the ground. Then he turned to the remaining doctor and stared at him coldly.

The man stuttered in French, then quickly reverted to English. His hands and arms were shaking in fear as he looked down at his friend who was now bleeding out at his feet.

"I … I, recommend cyanide. We have a healthy supply and can have it here by nightfall."

Sammy nodded his approval. "Good, I want it done by morning. No need to bury the dead. Just leave them." He turned to walk away and stopped. "Oh, one more thing. Don't speak that French crap to me anymore or I'll kill you. I don't like French."

The doctor nodded and spoke in perfect unbroken, English. "Yes, sir. I understand."

Sammy Thurmond, the man with Hannibal Lecter's voice walked away, all the while thinking, wondering *Am I on the winning side or the losing side?* He no longer knew for sure.

Sammy meets Jackie

SAMMY THURMOND HADN'T ALWAYS BEEN EVIL. IN fact, there had been a time, long, long ago when he'd been a good kid, some would say even exemplary. He'd gone to Sunday School, prayed to Jesus, and even been a boy scout for a time. Anamosa, Iowa had been a good place to raise a good kid. It was rural, conservative, a place where everyone knew everyone else and life was slow. Sammy had grown up playing on the banks of the Wapsipinicon River, a three-hundred-mile-long tributary of the Mississippi, full of catfish with a rocky bottom that always seemed to snag his lures and cost him plenty in fishing tackle.

Young Sammy could have been a preacher, or a school teacher, or maybe even a factory worker or farmhand on one of the nearby pig farms. But … that was not to be. As in so many other lives, the future of this small boy was altered by one event, one lone event, isolated from everything that had previously happened. Up until that one day, Sammy had been a good boy. But he'd been plagued with unacceptance. The other kids didn't like him and resisted his sincere and relentless overtures at friendship. They'd shunned him, not as a full-fledged pariah, but simply as someone a rung or two below them on the ladder of life. Sammy sensed this and would do anything to fit in. One day the other boys dared him to break the window of old man Garrison's garage. Sensing the opportunity for acceptance, Sammy hadn't hesitated.

After that one indiscretion, Sammy was no longer his own. He'd given up his freedom and his individuality for acceptance into the group. After that fateful day – they owned him. Breaking windows graduated to slashing tires, to setting fires, to reckless driving, to thievery. Finally, at age seventeen, Sammy was caught breaking into a convenience store. He'd stolen only a case of beer, but because of his past misadventures the judge came down hard, giving him the chance for prison time or enlisting in the military. He'd chosen the military and soon left Iowa behind forever.

One thing about Sammy Thurmond – he never looked back.

Sammy learned to kill in the army. In fact, he became very good at it. The act of killing fascinated him, so he practiced as often as he could and became proficient at its art. He was recruited by the CIA where he learned even more about killing and deviance and cunning. It was there, in the service of his country, where Sammy Thurmond's eyes turned cold-green and evil.

And by the time The Blind Man took notice of Sammy, he'd already killed hundreds of men, and any vestige of small-town Iowa had been rent from his soul. That had been ten years ago, and now Sammy was forty-five.

Sammy looked over at Jackie Branch now and smiled coldly. Now that she was cleaned up he could see how beautiful she was. They were inside his large tent. She was eating at the wooden picnic table while he looked on in a folding chair from ten feet away. She ate ravenously, like a wolf, and that only served to interest him all the more. Sammy listened intently to his self-talk and soon surmised his real interest in her was not her beauty, because he could have beautiful women at his beck and call. No, it wasn't that. He was surprised to learn that his interest in her was purely professional. Sammy was a cold-blooded killer by trade, but, sitting here in front of him, just a few feet away, was a woman who'd killed thousands in just a few day's time. And he respected that.

Jackie finished eating and looked over at him. "Do I have you to thank for the food and the clean clothes?"

Sammy didn't say anything. He simply nodded.

"Well then, thank you. I appreciate it."

Sammy nodded again. A year ago Jackie would have been terrified just being in the same room with this man, but so much had occurred to transform her, that she wasn't bothered by it. She could see the evil in his eyes, sense it more than see it. And it was obvious by his bearing and his demeanor that he was the most dangerous man in the room, wherever that room might be.

"Are you the one who ordered all the sick people to be killed?"

Sammy nodded and smiled.

"You realize you're doing my job for me?"

Sammy was wearing a black t-shirt with khaki tactical pants. There was a Glock model 22 strapped to his right hip with three extra mags on his left hip. His huge, muscular arms were wrapped around his massive chest tightly. But he didn't answer her.

"What's your name?"

Sammy narrowed his eyes slightly. "Names will not be necessary."

The coldness in his voice caused Jackie to shiver despite the stifling July heat and humidity. She forced a smile.

"I see. The strong, silent type."

Sammy felt amused and that fact surprised him, as he couldn't recall the last time he'd been amused. Jackie had been surprised to see the white, linen napkin beside the silver and china, but she picked up the linen now and lightly wiped her lips.

"What is going to happen to me?"

Sammy shrugged. "Life is precarious and unpredictable."

Jackie smiled at his remark. "Well, not as unpredictable as you might think." She forced herself to look into the man's cold, green eyes as she spoke. "I am going to die soon. It doesn't take a sage to figure that one out. The only question is 'Will I die with honor, as a tribute to my people?'"

She could tell her statement interested him.

Sammy uncrossed his arms. "Tell me please, what does it look like to die with honor?"

Jackie leaned forward and placed her elbows on the pine

picnic table. "It means that I die for a purpose I believe worthy … a purpose of my own choosing. It means that my own death helps the ones I love to survive and to fight on against evil."

Sammy nodded. "Yes. Altruism. I recognize that. It's the practice of unselfish devotion to others. I've killed many altruistic people."

Jackie held his gaze. "I believe you." Then she hesitated. She knew in her heart that Dan was out there watching the camp, that he would undoubtedly try to rescue her and that he would certainly die in the attack. "I wonder … perhaps … if you might do me one more favor."

Jackie let the request linger in the humid air of the tent. The man didn't answer, but she could tell he was still interested, so she continued. "I respectfully request that you kill me as quickly as possible."

Sammy Thurmond leaned forward in his chair. The Blind Man would like this woman. She was so polite. "And why would you like that? Don't you have something or someone to live for?" Sammy threw the words out like a piece of cheese tossed with purpose to a helpless and hungry mouse.

Jackie's eyes misted over, but she willed the tears to dissipate. "Sometimes dying for the ones you love is more important than living for them."

"Really? How so?"

She folded her hands and placed them under her chin. "Because, as long as I'm alive the attacks on this camp will not reconvene. And if this army is not destroyed, then the ones I love will eventually be killed. Logic therefore dictates that I die in order for the ones I love to live."

Now Sammy truly was amused, perhaps more than he'd ever been amused in his adult life. "You have a husband. Colonel Dan Branch. A baby named Donna. A step-son named Jeremy. These are the ones you love. And these are the reasons you kill?"

Jackie nodded. "I kill for them. And I die for them."

Sammy Thurmond stood up to his full six-feet, two-inch frame and slowly walked over to where Jackie was sitting. He unholstered his Glock as he went. Jackie didn't move. Upon feeling the warm metal against her ear, she turned and faced him. "I want to look my killer in the eyes. And I want you to know that I bear you no ill will."

Jackie's dark eyes met Sammy's cold, green gaze. Neither moved for almost a minute. Then, slowly, Sammy's finger began to take up slack on the trigger. Jackie waited, knowing she would never see Dan Branch again, wondering what woman would raise her child, believing that someday another woman would share the bed of her husband. She regretted that it had come to this, but her soul was at peace. She would die with honor.

Sammy Thurmond smiled and reholstered his pistol. "I will consider your request." And then he walked out of the tent, leaving Jackie alone with her love and her logic.

CHAPTER 20

July 8th, Uncle Rodney's Reconciliation

"**S**O WHAT'S IT GOING TO TAKE, young Daniel, to move you from the liability column back to the asset column?"

Dan Branch looked across the desk at his Uncle Rodney through bloodshot eyes. He hadn't slept in two days. "That's easy. Just take off these handcuffs. I'll do the rest."

Uncle Rodney looked over at the man he'd raised as his own son. He was proud of him, at his loyalty and bravery. But he was also disappointed at the boy's lack of logic and emotional self-control.

"Dan, you have to learn to control your emotions if you're going to have any hope of saving your wife."

Dan's eyes perked up. "You're going to save her?"

The old general looked tired and worn as he shifted in the plush, high-backed chair inside Colonel MacPherson's office.

"No, Daniel. I'm just a tired old man. I'm going to stay here in Escanaba. You're young and full of piss and vinegar. You're going to save her. After all, she's *your* wife."

Dan's shoulders slumped forward, letting his exhaustion show just a bit.

"Did you actually think I would let her die without even trying?"

The young man looked up into his general's eyes. Both men had suddenly softened their demeanor.

"I ... I, just wasn't sure. I've been in that cell for two days, and ... I know how you are."

Rodney's eyebrows lifted up. "Really? And how am I, young Daniel?"

Dan squirmed in the chair with handcuffed wrists on his lap. He hated it when he called him young Daniel. But he wanted to choose his words carefully. Angering the one man with the power to help him would do his wife no good.

"The mission is paramount. The mission is to defeat the Saracen army in battle and save Iroquois. You'll stop at nothing to achieve the mission ... even if it means sacrificing my wife to do it."

Uncle Rodney looked straight into his son's eyes. For a moment Dan thought he saw tears, but they quickly went away, immediately replaced with the hardness of granite and the heat of lightning.

"Anyone else's wife would already be dead, along with the rest of that Saracen rabble! I love Jackie, but she's alive because of you and only because of you."

Dan's eyes met his uncle's and they locked like the horns of a bull. "You would kill her yourself if it meant destroying the Saracens?"

Uncle Rodney nodded. "I certainly wouldn't ask someone else to do my own dirty work. Do you think she's the first casualty of war? Remember eighty-four-year-old Harold Steffens who died crashing his crop duster into two hundred enemy soldiers? Your wife helped him install the weapon's system on that plane. Harold died along with hundreds of others in the last battle. And Jackie knew going into this mission that is was a risk. She knew she could die, but she made that choice for herself, just like you make the choice every time you lead other men into battle. You're no different than I am and Jackie's no different than you and I. She risked her life to save her family. And why shouldn't she? She's as much a warrior as you and I."

Dan lowered his eyes. "I just ... it's just that ..." But he couldn't finish the sentence.

His Uncle Rodney stood up and walked around the desk. He went down to his knees and embraced his nephew. "I know. You don't have to say it."

Both men were quiet for a full minute. Then, Uncle Rodney stood back up and returned to his chair. "Here's the bottom line, Dan. I have a plan, but it requires no less than one-hundred percent of your cooperation and loyalty in order to succeed." He hesitated. "Are you willing to listen?"

Dan nodded. "Absolutely."

Rodney smiled softly. "Okay then. I need you to go to Ludington."

Dan's smile faded. "Ludington? How in God's name will that help Jackie?"

"Just hear me out, Dan."

General Branch filled him in on the details, and twenty minutes later Colonel Branch walked out of the office and boarded a helicopter headed for the Lake Michigan port city of Ludington in Mason county on the northwest coast of Michigan.

July 9, The Saracens on the Move

EVENTUALLY, THE DISEASE BURNED ITSELF OUT, AND the army was healthy once more and ready to move again toward Iroquois. Finally, the Saracen encampment packed up and moved forward once again, with Jackie Branch lashed tightly atop the wooden cross affixed to a Peterbilt semi-truck at the head of the column. Over three thousand of the sick had been executed and left to rot in the summer sun. The sound of buzzing insects feeding on the flesh could be heard even a hundred yards in the distance.

Supreme General Al'Kalwi stood atop his Bradley Fighting Vehicle and looked out across the expanse of his army and trembled with anger. He'd amassed thirty-thousand men, and they'd been reduced to only seventeen thousand in just a week's time. He was beginning to regret his agreement with The Blind Man. But ... he looked up at the sky above him, filled with Apache attack helicopters and fighter jets. What choice did he have? He hated kafirs! And the Blind Man was the infidel he hated the most. Sammy Thurmond was a close second.

He tried to put that out of his mind now. Before he could kill The Blind Man, he first had to defeat this Shadow Militia. At least now he had massive air support and added protection in the form of Jackie Branch, displayed on a cross for all to see. They would not dare attack him so long as she was there. In practical terms that meant all seventeen thousand of his army would make it safely to Iroquois City for the big battle. Seventeen thousand, along with heavy armor and air support would be more than enough to destroy the Shadow Militia army.

Sammy Thurmond had over-viewed the plan to him. All his army had to do was show up to draw out the Shadow Militia's airpower and armored forces, then The Blind Man would swoop in to destroy them all and all of Michigan would be under the Supreme General's command. He let go of his anger for a moment. It was a good start.

He studied the caravan. No more Humvees. Only two of the Strykers could be salvaged, and they'd lost two of their Abrams tanks to heat damage. He counted seven, eight-wheeled drive heavy duty trucks still operable as well as several dozen deuce and a halves. His lieutenants were already scouring the nearby truck stops and rest stops for semi-truck and trailer replacements. But, in the end, they still wouldn't have enough vehicles to haul their men and their equipment.

Sammy Thurmond had recommended moving his army in two stages. They were still over 150 miles from Iroquois, and that normally could have been travelled in a single day, but aerial recon had reported several overpasses had collapsed onto the freeway, and that would dictate time-consuming detours.

By the end of the first day they made it to Big Rapids, a city of just over 10,000 people before the day. There was a small airport there about two miles northwest of the city, and that's where the Saracen army made camp. Abdul had argued against it, but Sammy Thurmond's insistence, backed up by fighter jets and attack helicopters had persuaded him to go along.

July 10, Big Rapids,

JACKIE BRANCH SAT AT THE FOLDING TABLE WITH THE white plastic top inside the office room at the Roben-Hood Airport in Big Rapids. Her hands were duct-taped behind her, but at least she was off the cross for now. It had been like this for the past two days. At sundown she was taken off the cross to a tent or another secluded room where she would dine with Sammy Thurmond. The table was always set with a white linen table cloth, linen napkins, china and silver. On this particular evening there was a lit candle and, beside it on the table, was a red rose. Jackie had no idea where he'd gotten the flower, but she could smell it, so she knew it was real.

While Jackie was deep in thought, she heard the door knob turn. She looked up to see Sammy Thurmond walk in alone and close the door behind him. Two of his guards stationed themselves outside the door. They held the same M4A1 automatic carbines she frequently saw with Uncle Rodney's Shadow Militia details.

The Blind Man's assistant sat down in the chair opposite her and watched her silently from across the table. Jackie met his gaze and once again felt the evil there, but it was somehow softer than two days ago. Inside she admitted, *Why not? Even sociopaths can be chivalrous if they want to be?* She waited for him to speak.

"Would you like to eat now?"

Jackie hadn't had anything except water and some bread all day long, and she was famished. But she refused him.

"Not right now. I was hoping we could talk first. I always like a little before-dinner conversation."

The big man in front of her nodded slightly. "As you wish. Begin."

"A few days ago you told me that names were not necessary. Is that still the case?"

Sammy nodded. "Yes. When it changes, I will notify you."

Jackie smiled slightly. "You remind me a little of my husband."

Sammy Thurmond moved a bit in his chair. Jackie noticed this right away. Normally he remained coiled with mannequin -like stillness.

"I remember when I first met Dan in that cabin up in Wisconsin. He was so stoic. He rarely talked to me." She glanced out the window at the setting sun. There was no air conditioning or ventilation of any kind with the power out, but she had long ago acclimated to the severe heat. "Are all strong men so quiet?"

Sammy answered curtly. "No, not all. Some men talk too much."

"Well, sir, no one will ever accuse you of being a chatterbox."

Jackie turned back and met his gaze. His evil green eyes were almost smiling as he spoke. "Was that humor?"

Jackie laughed out loud. "Why, yes, I believe it was. A subtle brand of humor I think, but, humor, nonetheless."

She rubbed her wrists back and forth to get more circulation in her hands. "General Branch is similar to you as well."

Sammy Thurmond's eyes perked up. "Talk about General Rodney T. Branch."

Jackie smiled and nodded in acquiescence. "I could do that. A little anyways." And then she grew silent as she decided what to say and, more importantly, what not to say. She contemplated lying to him, but somehow sensed he would know. The last thing she wanted to do was anger this man. Despite his kindness, she knew he was still an unpredictable sociopath … and the enemy.

"Uncle Rodney is a gentleman, like yourself, but he's also very blunt, sometimes to the point of being rude. He tells the truth, even when I don't want to hear it. He is strong – very strong. And the only way to defeat him is to kill him." She paused a moment, contemplating the irony of her next comment. "I always get the impression he's the kind of man who opens the door for ladies with one hand while shooting his enemies with the other. He's an enigma I suppose."

Her captor lifted his right leg and crossed it over his left thigh. His arms were still folded across his muscled chest. Jackie waited, and finally he spoke. "I like him." There was silence. "And I respect him."

Jackie smiled. "Me too. Tell me why please."

Now it was Sammy Thurmond's turn to decide what to say and what not to say. If he killed her, then it wouldn't matter how much he told her. And, quite frankly, how could she possibly get away.

"If I was General Branch I would have used a sniper to shoot you while on the cross, then resumed killing the Saracen army. Why hasn't your general killed you?"

Jackie's eyes grew serious. She had wondered about it herself. In fact, she'd wished for death by sniper more than once while hanging helplessly on the wooden cross. She wouldn't have blamed Uncle Rodney for ordering her death, nor would she have thought less of Donny Brewster for carrying out the task, but … she couldn't help but wonder *Is my son watching me through his spotting scope? Does he have the crosshairs on me throughout the day?* She would not want her own son to do the job. It would be too much for him to live with – too high a price to pay with little chance of long-term healing.

"I think … because, Uncle Rodney is plagued by his own

humanity. His job is to kill, and he's very good at it. But ... when he kills, he kills with remorse, and only when it's necessary to defend innocence."

Sammy Thurmond uncrossed his legs. "But are you not innocent?"

The question jolted Jackie like a shock wave, rocking her head slightly back, and Sammy knew he'd hit onto something important. It was several seconds before she finally answered.

"No. Sin is familiar to me."

The big man leaned slightly forward. "Tell me your sin. I want to know."

For the life of her, Jackie couldn't begin to understand why this man would want to hear her confession, but he did.

"I would rather not, sir."

"Tell me your sin, and I will grant your wish."

Jackie squirmed back and forth in her chair. She didn't want to confess to this man. It had been different with Dan and Jeremy. They were worthy; they cared about her. But that knowledge was not safe with this man. He spoke again, this time with more firmness.

"Tell me your sin, and I will release you from your pain."

It would save the lives of her son, her daughter and maybe even her husband. So she obliged him.

"I cheated on my husband. I slept with another man. My husband is white, but my baby is black."

Sammy Thurmond nodded slightly and briskly got up from his chair without hesitation. He walked behind Jackie and pulled out a quick-opening knife with a 4-inch razor sharp blade. He quickly flipped it open and Jackie shuddered to herself *No, not with a knife. Not that way.* But she said nothing.

Sammy reached down behind her and cut away the duct tape on her wrists. He then walked over and rapped on the thick glass. He nodded to one of the guards and soon food was brought in. Jackie couldn't believe her eyes when she saw no less than ten appetizers being brought in by servants. It was an authentic Lebanese mezze. an arrangement of flat bread, hummus, olives, tahini, salad and yogurt. Jackie quickly prayed and then dug into the food. Sammy Thurmond watched her with interest, but that didn't deter her. She only paused long enough to thank him. After she'd finished her plate, more servants entered bearing a variety of fresh vegetables and eggs, all prepared authentically Lebanese. Five minutes after that came several courses of spiced lamb, sausages and then some fish.

Jackie slowed down but continued eating for as long as she could. Finally, she placed the last bit of flatbread on her plate and nodded to her captor.

"Thank you. How did you do this?"

Sammy didn't answer her question. He just stood up and walked behind her. He put new duct tape on her wrists, and, as he was bent down beside her whispered quietly into her ear. "Life is extremely precarious and unpredictable."

And then he stood up and motioned for the guards to enter.

CHAPTER 21

July 11, Donny Brewster's Frustration

DONNY BREWSTER, MASTER SNIP-
er, found it difficult to watch the Saracen army
without shooting them, but that's exactly what
he and his sixty-five other snipers had been doing ever since
Jackie had been captured. He was watching Jackie now from
over one thousand yards away in his hidey-hole. He studied
her face, and couldn't help but note how healthy she appeared
compared to just a few days ago. There had been a marked im-
provement ever since The Blind Man's assistant had arrived.

Several days ago General Branch had ordered him to lay
out a rescue plan, but so far he'd come up with nothing. The
enhanced security, complete with surveillance cameras, min-
iature drones and extra guards had made it all but impossible.

Donny hated the drones. They showed up at the most inop-
portune times, and they could get a man killed lickety split.
He'd already shot down two of them himself, but more just
kept coming. But, by far, the hardest task for Donny had been
explaining the situation to Jeremy Branch. As predicted, the
boy wanted to rush in with guns blazing on a rescue mission,
but Donny had forbid it. It was a suicide mission, and Donny
saw absolutely no hope, under the present circumstances, of
mounting a rescue. Inside he feared that Jackie Branch was already marked for death. As soon as the Saracen army reached

Iroquois city, Jackie would no longer be of any use, and they were but a day's ride away.

Major Jackson and the bulk of the harassing force had been called back to Iroquois the day before, so it was just Donny and a few of his snipers who were left here to observe and report. Down below the Saracens were packing up, getting ready for the final leg of their journey, and then they would be within striking distance of Iroquois. Dan knew that Sheriff Leif was coordinating the defenses, but had no idea about the details. Personally, unless the general had a trick up his sleeve, he didn't think the town could be held against these odds. If Jackie hadn't been captured, it would've been a different story, but ... she had. And that was a game changer. And, Donny Brewster, the Shadow Militia's most potent soldier was impotent. His hands were tied.

Iroquois City

"GET THAT TRUCK LOADED UP! EVERYTHING HAS TO BE ready by nightfall!" Sheriff Leif couldn't believe they were evacuating the town, that it had come to this. But, he'd agreed with General Branch, that it was the best they could do, and that no reasonable hope existed of successfully defending Iroquois City. Joe didn't like it, but they appeared to have no choice. As soon as nightfall set in they would sneak out of town and head north to rally with the other fighters from the surrounding counties of the North. Marge and his son had already left along with the rest of the outlying countryside.

For the past week Sheriff Leif had been traveling across the contiguous counties to call up their allies. To his surprise, most of them had agreed to rendezvous and stand with The Shadow Militia. Joe thought they were all crazy, but he kept his lack of faith to himself. In all, they would be able to assemble perhaps four thousand troops against the Saracen army of seventeen thousand, but they would not be able to prevail. In his God's-honest heart, Joe knew that.

Deep inside, he secretly hoped that Rodney Branch had a plan. In the last battle, he'd bet against Rodney and lost, but now ... it just seemed so hopeless. Even with the Abrams tank and Bradley fighting vehicles they'd salvaged from the last battle they were still outnumbered seventeen to one.

"Hey! Hurry it up there. Bobby, get those crates loaded up!"

And then he moved to the next truck and the next one after that. But he did so with a resolute doggedness, understanding that he'd placed his life and the entire town in the hands of a mad man. His only reassurance was the fact that he had no choice. His list of options was growing mightily thin. A sigh passed by his lips uncensored and he thought to himself, *Yes, Uncle Rodney was a mad man, but he was his mad man.*

Precarious and Unpredictable

THAT EVENING AFTER HER LUXURIOUS DINNER WITH Sammy Thurmond, Jackie Branch was placed back upon the cross. Her new captor had been more kind to her than the supreme general, had given her good food, medical attention, a new set of clothes, and had even given her hard-soled hiking shoes to wear while on the cross. But, unfortunately, he had not yet made good on his promise to kill her so that Dan and his Militia Rangers and Donny Brewster and his snipers would be free to attack the Saracen army.

Jackie's arms were duct-taped to the wooden crossbeams in such a manner that allowed her to move them just enough to stimulate circulation. The Supreme General had simply lashed her on with rough hemp rope causing abrasions to her skin which had become infected and swollen. They were almost healed now thanks to the medical attention authorized by Sammy Thurmond.

Jackie listened now to the sounds of the Saracen encampment as they set up and dug in for the night on the eve of battle. They had just finished the call to prayer over the loudspeakers, and men were moving again, going about their ways with various tasks. As far as Jackie could tell, the Saracens were nothing more than an organized rabble, held together by the consistent cruelty of one man: Supreme General Abdul Al'Kalwi.

But there were unexpected benefits to hanging on the cross surrounded by seventeen thousand people who hated you. Jackie was ready to die, was, indeed, at peace with it, and just waiting for it to happen. She felt a bit like the tribulation saints in the book of Revelation. She was dying for a cause and dying with honor in a way that would make her family proud of her. In that she had no regret.

Simply to be on this cross, two large barn beams dovetailed and spiked together, helped her to empathize with her own Lord, the one called Jesus Christ. It had forced her to take stock of her life, to get serious about her beliefs and to get her soul in order before her death. How many other people could say that? Most people in these violent and dangerous times died in a flash without the opportunity to clean up their spiritual house before they died. In that, she was lucky. Oddly enough, even though she hung on a cross, sure to die, surrounded by hate and rage, Jackie Branch was more at peace than at any other time in her life.

More importantly, Jackie, for the first time since cheating on her husband, felt forgiven. Not just forgiven by God, but forgiven by herself.

Jackie looked over at the surveillance camera staring down at her from the truck off to the left. She looked into it and smiled warmly.

A hundred yards away, sitting comfortably inside his command tent, Sammy Thurmond saw her smile and chuckled for the first time in decades. This woman, with her courage and forgiveness and peace, had opened a door inside him. It swung open on rusty hinges with a loud clank, and would never close again. It was, at the moment of her smile, when he decided to keep his promise. He would do it tonight while the rest of the camp slept in preparation for battle.

Yes, tonight he would set this brave woman's soul free.

CHAPTER 22

Ludington Harbor

CAPTAIN JOHN DARKFOOTE SAT IN his usual royal blue nylon stadium chair on the foredeck of the SS Badger as he watched the sun rise to its peak in the eastern sky over the small city of Ludington. There was a Beretta 92FS strapped to his hip and a 308 caliber hunting rifle leaning against the bulkhead just a few feet away. From the outset of The Collapse, most of the locals had respected his self-proclaimed lordship of the Badger, but for those who had not ... he was a pretty good shot with the 308.

Every once in a while some wayward soul would wander into the parking lot of the terminal and make his way toward the Badger. Usually, one or two warning shots would change their mind. The third shot was always center of exposed mass. In the ten months since The Collapse, John had allowed only one person to come aboard.

A sudden sharp pain hit him in the chest like a knife and he doubled over in the chair. He kept his head down, clutching his ribs with his right hand until the pain subsided. It was coming more frequently now, and he had no idea why it was happening. Whatever it was, it couldn't be good. After a few seconds the pain subsided, and he sat back up straight in his chair.

The harbor in Ludington was located inland on the Pere Marquette Lake at the mouth of a river bearing the same name. The lake itself was over 500 acres, with a channel that ran past the city marina on the right and the Harbor View marina just beyond it. After that it was a straight shot past the lighthouse and into lake Michigan.

John Darkfoote wasn't the real captain of the SS Badger. That man had left his post within twenty-four hours of The Collapse along with the rest of the crew. The others had family, so they'd hurried home, and John hadn't seen them since. John was the maintenance man, and he'd secured the stern gate and hosted the gangway on the ship two weeks after all hell broke loose. It had been a necessary task, and one that undoubtedly saved his life.

Those first few months had been extremely dangerous. On the day of The Collapse, the harbor had been a peaceful playland for the rich and famous, filled with yachts, parties and a congeniality where everyone knew it was safe to rest or play. John recalled that on the day after The Collapse many of the boats had left the harbor. The stupid ones, not willing or able to fathom the scope and terribleness of a world without electricity, returned to their homes in large cities like Chicago, Milwaukee and Detroit, only to fall prey to a brave new world void of police and public services. They quickly died. Others stayed in port and died of cold and starvation over the winter. Several had tried to storm the SS Badger late in the fall, desperate, cold, but well armed. John had shot them dead and left the bodies in the gravel parking lot as a welcome mat to anyone else with similar designs.

John wasn't an ordinary maintenance man. He'd served first in the army as a ground pounder, then sailed in the engineering department on ocean-going freighters in the merchant marine for twenty years. Then he'd taken the job on the Badger thinking he'd put down some roots, maybe raise a family, perpetuate his lineage. He'd thought wrong. There was no family. No woman. No kids. Not a single friend. Sure, there had been work friends on board, but … that was different.

During his past ten years on the ship. he'd learned everything he could about the Badger. He'd read all the manuals, watched the rest of the crew and asked incessant questions about the many mundane details of their job. He could fire up the Four Foster-Wheeler "D - type" coal-fired boilers, he could even start the engines. Each of the two Skinner Unaflow four-cylinder steam engines were rated at 3,500 horsepower at 125 RPMs. At the time of The Collapse, the SS Badger had been the only coal-fired steamship in operation in the United States. The SS Badger was a car ferry over four hundred feet long and almost sixty feet wide. Before The Collapse it ferried people, cars, trucks, motorcycles and RVs back and forth from Ludington, Michigan to Manitowoc, Wisconsin. The trip was sixty miles and took four hours each way.

"Here's your coffee, John."

The woman handed him the steaming glass mug and John accepted it readily. He blew off the steam and took a sip.

"You make good coffee, kid."

The woman was beautiful, in her late twenties, with long, auburn hair with natural waves that draped lazily over her bare shoulders. Her legs were long, slender and tan. She was wearing shorts and a sleeveless flowered-print blouse. If there had been anyone else on board, they'd have noticed how much younger she was than John. They'd notice her beauty and juxtaposed it to the plain, weathered face of her sixty-year-old partner. But they'd also have picked up on the chemistry and natural connection that seemed to flow between the two.

John had saved her life, and, despite the age difference and the disparity in attractiveness, she'd fallen in love with him. She hadn't meant to; it had just … happened … in the most natural way with no pomp or lead-up, not even the hint of romance. One minute they'd been friends, and in the next heartbeat they'd become lovers. And for the first time in his life, John Darkfoote had someone to talk to.

"We're running out of coffee, John."

John nodded. "I know. Coffee, sugar, rice, flour. We're running out of everything I suppose." He hesitated. "Well, we still have plenty of fish." He chuckled to himself.

She sat down in the wooden deck chair beside him. She lifted up her left leg and draped it over his right thigh. The softness of her skin made his thigh tingle.

"I suppose you want me to rub your feet again."

Eileen smiled. "You don't think I keep you around simply for your good looks and charming personality do you?"

John chuckled out loud.

"I suppose not." He took off her lime-green flip-flop and began to run his hand up and down her arch the way she liked it.

"So what are we going to do when we run out of food, John? I'm starting to get worried."

John didn't answer right away. In reality, he had no plan, no answer, but he didn't want to tell her that. In truth, John loved her too, and didn't want her to worry.

"I have a plan. We have forty state rooms that aren't being used. We could rent them out to summer tourists. We could advertise online, and we'll be rich in no time. Don't worry your pretty little head about it."

Eileen smiled at his humor. There was no such thing as tourism anymore. People didn't take vacations. There was no rest from work as work was the only buffer between starvation and the wolves at the door. She recalled the night most of the condos surrounding the harbor had burned down. It had been in December when people had started heating with wood. But the condos weren't designed for that. Without proper chimneys and ventilation and a fire department the condos had burned to the ground in one night. John and Eileen had watched all through the night as the heat from one condo ignited the roof and walls of the building beside it. Like dominoes they had all fallen as the strong wind fanned the flames of cold winter destruction. John and Eileen had the harbor pretty much to themselves now.

"Why did you save me, John? You could have let that man kill me, and no one would have known. I simply would have died and faded away."

John remembered the evening last fall when he'd heard the woman's scream. He'd watched as Eileen had run from the city marina to the parking lot beside the SS Badger. Then the man had knocked her to the ground unconscious and began to remove her clothing.

Usually John took the more forgiving center-of-mass shot, but this time, for some reason, he placed the crosshairs on the back of the man's head, level with the brain stem and slowly pressed the trigger to the rear. By the time Eileen had awakened, she'd been redressed, cleaned up and her head wound attended to.

John Darkfoote knew nothing of Eileen's past. He just assumed she had something shameful she wished to hide or something very painful she didn't want to discuss. If the former, then they were kindred spirits, because John had plenty of shame and had no right to judge. If the latter, then it was none of his business unless she volunteered it, and he wished her no pain in the recollection.

From a practical standpoint none of it mattered. She was a beautiful, young, intelligent woman who was healthy to boot who enjoyed his company and loved him. Before The Collapse society would have frowned on their union, but now … all bets were off. Society was destroyed, so people were left with two things: things that worked and things that didn't.

John and Eileen worked.

John Darkfoote leaned his head back, closed his eyes and took in the full force of the sun. "I know. You're a nuisance and a pain in the butt. I should have let you die, but… I don't know. I've always been a sucker for redheads, so I decided not to hold your youth, beauty and lack of experience against you."

The young woman placed her hand on his thigh and smiled through perfect white teeth. She squeezed and John immediately came alive below decks.

"Do you have any regrets, John."

He turned his head and looked her in the eyes. They were bright green and deep, like the waters of Lake Michigan.

"I regret we didn't meet sooner."

The woman let her leg drop down to the deck and moved to her knees between John's legs. She reached up with her slender fingers and cradled his weathered face while moving her lips up to his own.

"In all honesty, John. If we'd met much sooner, what I'm about to do to you right now would have been a felony."

John and Eileen slid down to the deck, basking in the July sunshine, oblivious their tenuous paradise was about to be shattered.

"What are they doing down there, sir?"

Colonel Dan Branch looked away and laughed out loud. "What does it look like they're doing! Move us away for a minute and give them a little privacy. Land us over there in that gravel parking lot."

Five minutes later the Huey's rotors had stopped spinning and all six of Dan's security detail had set up defensive positions around the parking lot in front of the SS Badger. Both the man and the woman were dressed and armed now, but neither pointed a weapon in their direction. Dan Branch, standing just outside the Huey, keyed the microphone before speaking. "Attention SS Badger, this is Colonel Dan Branch of the Michigan Shadow Militia, requesting permission to come aboard."

Five minutes later Dan stood in the sunlit passenger lounge beside Eileen and Captain John Darkfoote.

North of Iroquois City

Rodney Branch looked out at the rag-tag collection of humanity spread out before him in the state forest. Just a year ago they'd all been farmers, factory workers, school bus drivers, stay-at-home moms, with maybe a few small businessmen, doctors, lawyers and accountants thrown in just for good measure. Even at four thousand strong, they were no match for the seventeen thousand Saracens headed their way.

But it wasn't the army of Christian-hating Saracens that bothered Rodney the most; it was the fighter jets and attack helicopters flying combat air patrol overhead that seemed to seal their fate. Sheriff Leif was a good man, but he still didn't grasp the full scope of what was going on here. Rodney knew that Joe Leif resented the fact that he wouldn't throw all the Shadow Militia's forces, including airpower, into this one fight, but … if he did that … it would be over. He'd be playing into the Blind Man's hands, effectively giving him control of all North America.

And Rodney couldn't do that. This battle they were about to fight was just the beginning, just the precursor, the warm-up to an entire war that had to happen before all this madness and death would end. Rodney, sitting alone inside the cab of his F-250 pick-up truck, sagged his head. But, in his heart, he knew that madness never ended, that senseless death never ceased. Any student of human history could see that. Because life was a constant struggle of good fighting evil, and that's where Rodney came in. He liked to think he was the good guy, but … sometimes he wondered. Sometimes he doubted his abilities and his motives and his … his own goodness.

So far very little had gone right in their battle against the Supreme General. Jackie Branch had killed thousands, but then … if only she hadn't been caught. But it was senseless to regret the fate of things, actions of others, events outside his control. And right now so much seemed beyond Rodney's influence.

He knew what the Blind Man was doing, and he both hated and respected him for it. The Blind Man, however evil and twisted, was a worthy opponent. And he seemed to hold most of the cards. Jared Thompson's forces were stretched thin by all the guerilla fighting going on in the South, the West, and the Midwest, so he'd recruited the Saracens to do his dirty work.

Rodney was well aware of his own weaknesses, and, apparently, so was the Blind Man. Jared Thompson knew that Rodney would stand and protect his home, even if it meant defeat and certain death. But Rodney knew his own heart, knew that he could never abandon his friends and his neighbors, just as knew that he couldn't allow Jackie to die all alone on that wooden cross.

Tactically speaking, he should have kept attacking the Saracens even though it would have resulted in her death. If he had, they undoubtedly could have killed thousands more of the approaching army. Strictly from a tactical standpoint, he should have moved ahead of the Saracens as they pressed north. He should have burned every town along the US 131 corridor, thereby denying them the ability to scavenge for food and supplies. That would have been the sound, military decision.

As with all men, Uncle Rodney's greatest strength was also his greatest weakness.

Rodney recalled his decision to seek out help from God and winced. Prayer was something people did when all hope was gone, when their plans failed; it was an act of desperation. But, truth be known, Rodney was indeed desperate.

General Branch looked at the setting sun through his windshield. In the next few days people were going to die. He knew that. But, what he didn't know was that Dan Branch was now in Ludington, and that he'd secured the SS Badger.

A Soul Set Free

IT WAS NIGHT IN THE SARACEN ENCAMPMENT. TOMORROW was the battle, so Supreme General Abdul Al'Kalwi had ordered sleep for his rowdy warriors. As Jackie hung on the cross from her arms, fading in and out of restless sleep, she could sense the difference. She didn't know the area south of Iroquois simply because she had never been here before. But she sensed they were getting closer. All day long, last-minute preparations had been made all around her. People scurried like mice, loading trucks, cleaning rifles, packing bags, all the things that happened before men went into battle.

Jackie raised her head with a great deal of effort and looked up into the darkened sky. Ever since The Day when the power had gone out, the nights had seemed so much darker. She could see the stars with more clarity. There was the Big Dipper straight ahead of her. She followed the two pointer stars in the end of the cup until she found Polaris, the North Star. She stared into it and smiled. She thought about baby Donna, pictured her beautiful face, then regretted that she'd left her for the glories of war, which had turned out to be so incredibly inglorious after all was said and done.

If only she'd run for the woods on the day she'd been caught and placed on this cross. They might have shot her in the back; but she might have made it to the tree line. She could have been with her daughter right now, with her husband.

Jackie looked back down at the ground below her. Regrets were so … unproductive.

Lost in her own thoughts, Jackie didn't notice the man climbing up the side of the semi-trailer to where her cross was lashed. But she heard the soft footsteps behind her, and a wave of adrenaline surged through every inch of her body. When she felt the man's breath on her neck, her muscles tightened. Then he reached around and placed the steel blade against her throat. Her first thought was *No! Not the knife. I wanted a bullet to the brain. So much easier, so much quicker.*

"Good evening, Ms. Branch."

The voice was a deadly whisper, a guttural spew. She shivered in the July heat and humidity, taking a few seconds to master her fear before answering.

"Good evening, sir."

She knew who it was, who it could only be.

"Do you know why I'm here?"

Jackie looked back up at the stars. She followed the line formed by joining the pointer stars with Polaris and found Cassiopeia and thought *How beautiful. There are worse ways to die.* At least here she had the backdrop of God and all His creation.

"You are a man of honor. You've come to fulfill your promise."

Sammy Thurmond laughed softly.

"Yes. You know me better than The Blind Man."

And then he paused. "I'm going to miss you Jackie." The knife pressed a little harder against her throat. "I so much enjoyed our dinners and our talks."

Jackie, looking up at the Big Dipper, forced herself to answer softly. "Yes, you made an otherwise terrifying experience, memorable and thought-provoking."

For a moment Sammy was silent, then she felt the sharp blade move away from her throat and then down her shoulder and the length of her arm.

"There is a small group of your snipers to your immediate left just inside the tree line about five hundred yards. I don't know where your husband is."

The knife blade cut easily through the duct tape on her right arm. It immediately fell to her side limp. It took a few seconds for the blood to return. Within just a few moments the blade had also freed her left arm and then her waist followed quickly by her feet.

"You may turn around now."

Slowly, Jackie turned. Sammy's face was hidden in the shadows of a hooded Islamic robe. He placed the knife back in its sheath on his waist. Even in the starlight his eyes looked cold and green.

"You're letting me go?"

Sammy's face remained stone-cold as he spoke. "Take this

back to General Branch. Do not open it. Place it only in his hands."

Jackie reached out her right hand. Sammy Thurmond placed a plastic tube in her palm. It was about six inches long and an inch in diameter, and made of white, PVC pipe.

Jackie's fingers wrapped around the pipe. When she touched Sammy's skin, she was surprised to feel warmth emanating from his hand. She lingered there for a moment.

"I owe you my life."

"You owe me nothing. I make my own choices."

Jackie seemed confused by the coldness in his voice. It was out of place. This was a tender, intimate moment, but then she realized … it was the tenderness of assassins.

"Thank you, sir."

He then handed her a hooded sweatshirt and a small knapsack. She quickly put on the shirt and donned the pack.

"You have to hurry."

Jackie started to walk past him, but then stopped. She slowly reached out and embraced him. She felt his body tense and knew that the knife was already back in his hand on instinct alone. It was the reflex action of a highly trained killer.

She was reminded of the first time she'd hugged Uncle Rodney, and suddenly realized the two men were cut from the same basic cloth, however, different they'd turned out to be.

She moved back to arm's length, gave him one last look and turned to leave. But she was stopped dead in her tracks with his words.

"My name is Sammy."

From six feet away, Jackie turned and smiled.

"Thank you … Sammy."

Then she turned, made her way down the semi-trailer and filtered out into the camp before making her way to the tree line.

Sammy Thurmond reached up with both hands and moved the hood back to reveal his face. Then he watched until she was out of sight.

CHAPTER 23

"**I CAN'T BELIEVE I'M LETTING YOU** do this to my ship."

Dan Branch smiled at Captain John Darkfoote as the two men walked along the pier toward the lighthouse. As always, Dan's security detail was spread out all around him, some in plain view while others were hidden. They could hear the sound of semi-trucks backing into the cargo deck under the recently raised stern gate of the SS Badger off in the distance. So far ten trucks had arrived with more on the way. The Badger was being loaded for war.

"The plan has better than a fifty-fifty chance of success. These days those are pretty good odds." He hesitated for just a moment. "Besides, I'm sure Uncle Rodney has a back-up plan in case this doesn't work."

John Darkfoote ran his fingers through his thinning gray hair from front to back before answering. "Actually, I was kind of hoping for better odds than that."

Dan shrugged. "This is war, captain. Odds are we'll all be dead by this time next week anyway. The best we can hope for is to die with honor." Dan hesitated, looked down for a moment and then back up again.

"What's wrong, Dan?"

"Nothing. I was just thinking about my wife."

John looked off the pier into the lake. The water was dark blue today. "Where is she? Home?"

Dan looked out at the water now too, but his gaze was different than John's. It seemed to reach out further, all the way to the Wisconsin shoreline.

"Last I knew she was tied to a wooden cross being paraded in front of seventeen thousand blood-thirsty jihadis."

Captain Darkfoote didn't know how to respond. Normally he would assume the statement was some kind of sick joke, but Colonel Branch didn't seem like a joker, and his somber tone and sad eyes spoke louder than his words.

"You're serious. I can see that." He stopped walking for a moment. Dan followed suit, then started up again as soon as John moved forward. "That has got to be the first time in human history anyone has made that exact comment."

A flock of sea gulls flew overhead. Back before The Day birds like this would flutter over the hundreds of tourists, looking for free hand-outs. But those days were past, and now even the birds had to work for a living.

"Not really. Humanity has always been a cruel story. Good always fighting against evil. When evil wins then innocent people suffer and die. When good wins, there's a short-lived respite and a few days of peace. But the one constant has always been that evil never gives up, and it just keeps coming back at you generation after generation. No rest. Peace is a fleeting illusion – like smoke that rises up and is quickly blown out of reach."

John felt the wind on his face. It was hot but felt good nonetheless. "Well, Colonel, it was peaceful before you got here."

Dan forced a brief smile. He recalled the sight of two people making love on the foredeck of the Badger upon their arrival. "Yeah. Sorry about that." Dan looked out to the lake and then back to watch his feet as they fell to the cement … heel, toe … heel, toe … heel, toe – over and over again like some ghastly military machine that never gave in. "How long does it take to steam from here to St. Ignace?"

John Darkfoote thought for a moment. "Maybe twelve hours, give or take."

Dan stopped walking. He turned and faced John. "I need precision. You have to arrive at exactly the right moment or a lot of the wrong people will die."

Captain Darkfoote met Dan's stare. He reached up and stroked his chin nervously. "If that's the case then I recommend we make the trip in two stages. We could do the lion's share of the trip over night, maybe anchor at Beaver Island and then do a quick run in from the west. It's a lot more predictable that way, and less things can go wrong."

Dan thought a moment and then nodded his agreement. "That's a good plan. Thanks."

They both stood there on the pier, clumsily waiting for the other to speak again. Finally, Captain Darkfoote gave in. "So, Colonel, when are you going to tell me what's in all those trucks we're loading onto the Badger?"

Dan smiled and looked down at the cement. "It's a surprise captain – a really big surprise, and I don't want to spoil it for you."

John's eyes narrowed. "And you say I'll be handsomely compensated for my efforts?"

John nodded. "I'll work it out with the general. If we pull this off you'll be a hero and you can pretty much write your own ticket." Dan paused. "Of course, there is a risk – maybe a big risk. It all depends on how our enemies respond. I have to be honest with you, John. This isn't a milk run. You're not moving cars from Ludington to Manitowoc anymore."

They both turned and started walking back to the SS Badger. "All right then. As soon as you're loaded, then we can get underway. I'll need six of your men to help me sail though, and a few mechanics to help me get her ready. You promised me that."

Dan nodded. "Of course. Not a problem."

When the two men reached the parking lot, they shook

hands and parted. Dan boarded the Huey, and John went back to his ship to prepare for departure. The captain felt uneasy about the lack of details to this plan, but it also excited him. Finally, after ten months of sitting around, he was doing something useful. But he couldn't help but wonder about the danger. In the end he concluded it was better to die in glorious battle in a just cause than to starve to death in port.

Seven Miles South of Iroquois City

A YEAR AGO JEREMY BRANCH WOULD BE CRYING, BUT now ... he couldn't bring himself to do it. He had killed so many people. True, they were bad people, and, as Uncle Rodney was quick to remind him "They needed killing." But, still ... he was just a boy of sixteen. And now, they had his mother captive. He knew they were torturing her and ... God knows what else. He'd seen her several times through his scope. He wanted to rescue her, but he didn't know how. He had the courage, but not the know-how. He'd spoken to Donny about it, and was not encouraged. Not even Donny knew how to save her.

So they waited and they watched ... helplessly from the trees.

Jeremy was alone right now, taking a break from his listening post position. He was allowed a fifteen-minute break every four hours and his shift was twelve hours long. Every day he watched. Every day he did nothing to help his mother. The inactivity was killing him inside. He hadn't seen his father in days now. Donny said he was on a special mission for General Branch, but didn't know the details. Jeremy just wanted to go back home to Wisconsin, to the way things used to be before he'd killed those men. But ... deep in his heart ... he knew that was impossible. Even if God turned back the hands of time, Jeremy Branch had been changed forever. He was a man now, forever longing to return to boyhood.

He looked up and stared at the tree in front of him. It was

167

an oak, solid, unmovable, unrelenting to all but the very strongest of winds. It was one of the hardest woods in the forest, never bending and seldom breaking. Somehow, over time and action, Jeremy Branch had transformed from a willow to an oak. And he didn't entirely like it.

A twig snapped fifty yards into the woods and Jeremy jumped up, raising his M4 to his shoulder facing the threat. It was the same carbine his Uncle Rodney had given him. The sound was between his location and the camp. He peered through the night vision scope and saw nothing but trees. The sound was still coming though, so he followed it with the scope. Finally, a human form stepped out from behind a tree and Jeremy rested the crosshairs onto the center of the intruder's body. Jeremy moved his finger down until it rested lightly on the trigger. The form was now only twenty yards away and moving toward him. Following protocol, Jeremy issued the challenge. "Halt!" The form stopped immediately. Jeremy issued the password challenge. "Orion's belt!"

There was a short silence. Jeremy's finger took up slack in the trigger.

"Jeremy? Honey, is that you?"

Upon hearing Jackie's voice, Jeremy lowered his carbine. "Mom?"

The two rushed forward and embraced. All the tears the young man had been holding back now rushed out. His M4 rested lightly on the one-point sling between them as Jackie caressed his head. It was dirty, filled with black dirt and crushed pieces of dead bark, but she didn't care.

"It's okay, son. I'm fine. You'll be okay too. Go ahead and let it out."

And Jackie cried too, both of them together on the outskirts of the Saracen encampment. For a full five minutes they hugged quietly except for their tender whimpers. Then the silence was suddenly broken by a man working his way toward them in the darkness. Jackie and Jeremy quickly separated. Jeremy crouched down behind an oak tree in a defensive posture and issued the challenge. "Orion's Belt!"

Donny Brewster stopped walking and confirmed the challenge. "Maple tree."

When Donny stepped out into the small clearing, he saw the two and sucked in a surprised gasp of air.

"What?"

He rushed forward and gave Jackie a brief hug.

"Hurry! Follow me. We have to get out the word!"

All three of them moved quickly and quietly through the woods. In a matter of minutes General Branch was given the good news, and a new plan was formed.

July 13, the Saracen Camp

"DO YOU DENY IT WAS YOU WHO FREED THE PRISONER?"

"Yes, Supreme General! Of course I do. It was not me. And I have witnesses to prove it!"

Abdul's second in command was barely standing in front of him, quivering in fear before the power of his master, the Supreme General.

"Where were you last night?"

The lieutenant answered quickly and with forced and mock confidence. "I was with my women, sir. I was honoring them with my pleasure."

Abdul smiled inside, but remained stern. They were both standing in front of the white, plastic folding table with the laptop computer sitting on top of it. Sammy Thurmond stood quietly off to the side in a parade-rest stance of non-interference. The Supreme General reached down and pressed a button. The surveillance video began to play silently. The video was a little grainy, but clear enough for some measure of detail.

The lieutenant watched silently as a man walked up behind the infidel woman on the cross and whispered to her. Then he watched as she was set free with a knife. The man's face was shrouded in the shadows of a hooded robe. The woman turned

169

around to face the man who had freed her. She was handed a small piece of white plastic pipe followed by a sweatshirt and a knapsack. The woman quickly donned first the shirt, and then the pack. She started to walk away but then stopped and hugged the man who had just cut her loose. She turned and walked away again, then stopped once more to turn around. The camera angle was from the back. Then she walked out of the picture. The man in the hooded robe stood there watching after her. And then, the lieutenant's pulse quickened in his chest as the man in the video reached up and pulled the hood back revealing his face.

The second in command gasped out loud as he saw a perfect replication of his own face. All the strength in his legs left him as he fell down to his knees before the Supreme General.

Abdul reached down and pressed a button to pause the video.

"Do you still deny the evidence?"

The man on his knees started to cry and saliva ran freely from his mouth and onto the bare ground. He tried to talk, but could manage only a series of blubbers.

The Supreme General unsheathed his curved sword, and, with one swift, perfect stroke, the man's head flopped off and onto the ground. Blood gushed up for a few seconds, then lessened and stopped as the man's body collapsed beside the head.

"You were a good man, a good servant of Mohammed, peace be upon him. So I grant you mercy."

Then he motioned with his hand to the soldiers standing around him. "Take his body and bury it along with all those living in his household. Spare none."

Sammy Thurmond watched without passion as the man's body was dragged away. But he was smiling inside, lauding the praises of Jackie's escape, and the miracle of Photoshop.

July 13, Boyne City, Michigan

GENERAL RODNEY BRANCH STOOD IN THE CENTER OF the barn surrounded by thirty men. Some were standing, but the ones near the front were seated in the straw on the barn floor. Despite the heat and humidity, the barn doors were closed and guarded. When Rodney spoke, he did so in hushed tones, as if reading aloud from some top secret document.

"The Saracens have entered Iroquois City, and are presently camped there. We await their next move."

Rodney's words hung in the thickness of the July humidity for all to see and hear. They were solemn words. Sheriff Leif held his breath without realizing it. It was anticipated, as it turns out, even necessary, but ...

"From this point out, our main mission is to lead the Saracen army up from Iroquois all the way to Mackinaw City. While we lead them, the snipers and the Militia Rangers will operate in small independent groups of no more than four-man fire teams. Under no circumstances are you to form up into a cohesive force. The Saracens enjoy total air superiority which includes sophisticated infrared imaging technology. If you bunch up they'll kill you in a heartbeat. The F-18s and the Apache gunships now flying air cover are capable of destroying our entire force in a matter of minutes."

General Branch paused to let it sink in. "Our force of four thousand soldiers is all that stands between the Saracens and the straits of Mackinaw. Over the next few days we'll be attacking them with a series of uncoordinated hit-and-run movements." He looked out at the thirty or so leaders. He knew what they were thinking. *This is crazy. This is hopeless. We're all going to die.*

He needed them to be brave. He needed them to instill boldness in the ones they commanded. That had always been the job of the best field commanders. He needed to give them hope and blind courage.

"The Shadow Militia will destroy the F-18s as well as every last Apache attack helicopter. But first, you must lead them to Mackinaw City. If you get them there, we can do the rest." He paused trying to make eye contact with as many as possible. "You have to kill as many of them as you can, while keeping your own casualties to a minimum."

General Branch paced a few steps to his right, turned and then moved back to the left. "Are there any questions?"

Rodney watched as a few men looked at each other with uncertainty. Then he saw a hand rise near the back.

"Yes, you in the back."

General Branch was surprised to see Sergeant Donny Brewster step out from behind a group of three lieutenants. Last he knew the sergeant was still watching the Saracen army at Iroquois City.

"General, I'm just a non-com, so I want to make sure I got this right."

The general smiled.

"You want small groups of four people to attack a superior force of seventeen thousand soldiers while they're being protected by F-18 fighter jets and Apache attack helicopters, and we're not allowed to die in the process?"

General Branch nodded.

"And that's what I like about you, general. You keep things simple."

There was a chorus of hushed laughter as Donny sat back down and the general smiled again.

"I would think, Sergeant Brewster, that a Marine Corps sniper, backed up by flank protection on three sides is more than a match for seventeen thousand Saracens."

Donny Brewster jumped up and yelled as loud as he could "Oorah! You got that right, general! When do we start!?"

Up near the front of the crowd, Sheriff Leif shook his head in disbelief. Rodney Branch was a megalomaniac. Donny Brewster was crazy. And they were all going to die.

CHAPTER 24

July 13, Iroquois City

SUPREME **G**ENERAL **A**BDUL Al'Kalwi stood at the top of the old red brick courthouse inside the clock tower looking out across the town of Iroquois City. He'd won the battle without firing a shot, and his enemies had fled before him. They were terrified of him and his army, and wisely so. The men beside him were setting up the speakers just in time to broadcast the next call to prayer.

But Abdul was not happy with the easy victory. Earlier in the campaign he'd welcomed the addition of airpower to his army, but now … the F-18s and Apache helicopters flying overhead had become less of a comfort and more of a thorn in his side. The Supreme General now understood that he was but a tool, a detail in the larger plan of the Blind Man, who was simply an infidel with more powerful toys than Abdul.

Supreme General Abdul Al'Kalwi was being used. And he didn't like it. Unfortunately, he had no idea how to fix it. The F-18s and the attack helicopters had the ability to kill everyone in his army with but a nod from his adversary, the Blind Man. And now, he'd been forced to kill yet another of his lieutenants. That may have been a mistake. He couldn't get the nagging question out of his mind: *Why had his trusted lieutenant betrayed him? Why had someone so smart pulled back the hood and shown his face to the surveillance camera when he knew full well it was there?* But Abdul had been giv-en no choice. The others had seen the video, and if he hadn't killed him the word of his weakness would have spread across the camp.

Yes, he'd done the right thing, but ... he'd had no choice. And that's what he didn't like. Everything was being forced upon him by the Blind Man and his sociopathic pet, who was even now looking at him from the courtyard. More than any-thing Abdul wanted to kill the Blind Man. But ... *you can't kill what you can't see.*

That thought lingered and the irony was not lost on him. But there was no denying the fact of how he felt. He felt cor-nered, trapped and used. *Yes*, he thought to himself ,*The first chance I get I will kill the Blind Man and his crazy assistant. By myself it is impossible, but with the help of Allah it can be done.*

But first ... the Shadow Militia. He must catch them and kill them ... to the last man, woman and child.

Reunited

"You should have let them kill me, Uncle Rodney, or maybe even killed me yourself. Now, they have overrun the town and they're still coming. You could have been killing them all this time but ..."

General Branch raised his hand to silence her and baby Donna reached out and grabbed his finger. She placed the big callused digit in her mouth and began to bite down. She'd been teething in a major way.

"No, Jackie. I made a mistake and you almost paid for it with your life. And the rest of us ... well, we could all die because of that one mistake. Such is the way of war. When generals err – people die."

"You put too much on yourself, Uncle Rodney. I insisted, and wouldn't have accepted a 'no' answer from you. Don't forget that I was a very eager volunteer."

Jackie was wearing blue jeans and a gray t-shirt and they both were sitting on the ground with their backs against the same huge oak tree in the small township park. Baby Donna struggled to get loose now, and Uncle Rodney set her down on the bare ground.

"Perhaps. But the truth is I made a mistake. I didn't know myself as well as I thought I did. I thought I could allow you to die but I could not. The Blind Man knew that. He knows me better than I know myself."

Rodney lowered his head and sighed. "I have to do better or we're all dead and the world is enslaved."

Jackie laughed out loud. She covered her mouth with her hand in an effort to stifle herself, but couldn't manage it. "You men are all alike! Dan is the same way, putting the weight of the whole world on his shoulders, pretending that everything rises and falls on the actions of one man." She paused. "It's absurd! You realize that don't you?"

Uncle Rodney leaned his head back against the solidity of the giant oak tree, gaining strength and resolve from its ancient bark. The tree had seen Ottawa Indians and a world without telephones and computers, and in its wood lingered a wisdom and a point of view that had wrongly passed from all knowledge.

"I'm not responsible for what other men do. I'm only responsible for what I do. You're right. I should have killed you, but I didn't. The Blind Man saw the weakest part of my character and he used it for his own nefarious gain."

Jackie laughed out loud again. "Did you just say 'nefarious?' I can't believe you said that. It sounds like something from a cheap detective novel."

She reached over and gave him a hug. Rodney accepted it but still looked around to make sure no one was looking. Immediately, Jackie was reminded of Sammy. She reached into the knapsack beside her and pulled out the white plastic pipe that she'd been given on her release.

"This is for you." And then she told him the whole story of

her escape. Uncle Rodney questioned her relentlessly about Sammy Thurmond, and then she was questioned again and again by Special Agent Jeff Arnett until she could no longer stand it. All the while, she just wanted to be reunited with her husband. But ... at least she was alive and baby Donna was in her arms.

The SS Badger Leaves Port

CAPTAIN JOHN DARKFOOTE STOOD ON THE BRIDGE OF the SS Badger. They had just left Ludington Harbor and were now making their way up Lake Michigan. After seeing all the cargo inside the big trucks, he now understood what was expected of him ... and it chilled his soul.

He had a skeleton crew of eight people on board, and they were dead reckoning without GPS or radar or any other modern navigational aids. He was reminded of the mariners of old who'd sailed these waters a hundred and fifty years before his birth. At least they'd had help from the many lighthouses that dotted the western coastline of Michigan. But those were dark now, extinguished, perhaps for all time.

He would reach Beaver Island before dawn with just enough time to anchor and spend the day making preparations for his final run into the Mackinaw straits.

John's mind was lost now in thought and introspection. He had so many regrets, but at least now, at the very end of his life, he was willing to admit it. His few months with Eileen, his ecstasy with her, the extreme happiness of opening up to a woman and joining souls had helped him realize how foolish he'd been to choose a life of loneliness.

If he had the chance ...

But he didn't. His was a life heralded with waypoints of regret and nothing could change that now. John Darkfoote had missed the important things in life, traded them all away for a life of stoic sadness.

Just then Eileen entered the dimly lit wheelhouse, and

shuffled over to John in the near dark. She liked it up here at night, with only the green glow of the instruments. She hugged him from behind. "It's so beautiful out there in the darkness, isn't it, John."

John smiled and turned to take her in his arms. This young, beautiful woman was the pinnacle of his life, the one way-point without regret. And he was about to set another.

"Would you like to steer the boat, my dear?"

Eileen smiled and they both looked out into the darkness, facing it head on together.

Cicadas in the Trees

It was dark now, and Jackie lay peacefully in her husband's arms on the eve of battle. How many more times would she be forced to contemplate his death? Once again she was reminded of Sammy Thurmond ... of his ominous words "Life is extremely precarious and unpredictable."

But tonight it was a little different because she understood how Dan felt. She knew it wasn't all glory now, that it wasn't fun, that he was going out there and fighting not for his own glory, but for the lives and freedom of his family. She would do her part, but never again would she long for the glory of battle. That was an illusion that most people discovered only at the time of their passing.

"Dan? Are you asleep?"

She spoke softly so as not to disturb him if he was sleeping. She heard him chuckle softly. "Not anymore, dear."

She sighed. "Sorry honey."

"That's okay. They'll be plenty of time to sleep after I die."

She squeezed the hair on his chest and he winced. "Don't say that, Dan! Not tonight!"

"No problem. Just ease up on the chest hair will you?"

Jackie smiled in the darkness.

"So what were you thinking about, Dan?"

"I was asleep. I wasn't thinking about anything."

177

"So you have a flat brain wave? You can't do that, Dan. I'm your wife. I own you. Anything you think and anything you feel belongs to me."

Dan smiled. "And I feel lucky to be owned by such a benevolent master." He paused. "I just wish she'd let me get some more sleep. Especially on the eve of the battle of all time."

Jackie's fingers interlaced with his chest hair and squeezed again. He grimaced but remained silent.

"There is no such thing as the battle of all time, because there will always be another battle. The next battle will always be bigger, more paramount, more pressing than the previous." She hesitated. "Does it ever end, Dan?"

For a few seconds there was no answer. Dan listened to the cicadas high in the trees; their constant buzzing was the backdrop for all of northern Michigan during the month of July.

"No, honey. It never ends." He hesitated before going on. "But ... it does pause, and we live for those pauses, those brief respites from pain and suffering. And, it's during the pause that we live most of our lives. During the pause we meet a woman we love. We marry. During the pause we have children and we love them." Jackie listened intently. She'd never heard him talk like this before." It's the pause that we live for, and the pause that we ... die for."

Jackie hadn't told him all that had gone on during her capture, but ... Dan knew. He sensed the change in her. The pain. She chose to leave it behind her in the past, and Dan was wise enough and compassionate enough to allow her that luxury. In his mind, Jackie, his wife, was a hero.

"Will Uncle Rodney's plan work?"

Dan sighed and pulled her closer. "I don't know. It's too complicated for my tastes. His too I think. If one thing goes wrong then ..." He stopped in mid-sentence. "It doesn't matter. I'm with you right now. Let's just enjoy the pause and contemplate our new baby. What are we going to name him?"

Jackie raised her head up off his shoulder. Her black hair

cascaded down onto his chest. "Him?"

Dan smiled. "Of course. You're going to give me a son. Didn't I mention that?"

"But what if it's a girl?"

Dan reached over with his right hand and tenderly stroked her long, black hair. "If she's a girl, well, then let's just hope she's not as flat-out, butt-ugly as you are."

Immediately she rolled over on top of him and started pounding his chest with her fists. Dan laughed and grabbed her by the arms and reversed positions until he was on top of her, his body between her legs. And then ... he came down on her. She stopped struggling, grabbed the short blonde hair on the back of his head and moved up to kiss him with all the force of passion she could muster.

And, in that pause, with life growing inside her, on the eve of battle, while the cicadas buzzed their incessant backdrop, the two of them made wild, passionate love.

CHAPTER 25

July 14, The Deadly Prelude

THE SNIPERS FIRED THEIR FIRST volleys at dawn of the next day. Sergeant Donny Brewster took his mission seriously like no other, and hundreds were killed by his marksmen just north of Iroquois City. Then in the afternoon, further down the road, Major Larry Jackson attacked with more grenade launchers killing several hundred more. Undoubtedly he could have inflicted more damage if he hadn't run out of grenades.

That first day was a lot like the battle for Lexington-Concord on April 19th, 1775 when the British regulars were cut to ribbons on the road back to Boston. This time the airpower did little to stop the Militia Rangers as they seldom traveled in groups larger than two. They had taken General Branch's orders seriously, and this rendered the Supreme General's airpower almost useless to counterattack.

The Blind Man realized that every ounce of fuel burned, every missile launched and every bullet fired, was irreplaceable, at least for the next couple years until he could pacify and restore order to the country. Only then would he be able to build the country's manufacturing capability back to some semblance of its original power.

So the Supreme General was forced to endure the lone wolf attacks and suffer losses. On the second day, just north of Mancelona, the Saracen army discovered that small sections of the road north had been removed by diggers during the night, forcing the Saracen army to make costly detours. Many times those detours funneled the army into natural killing zones in the form of cedar swamps from which the snipers and rangers could pick a target at their leisure and shoot for much longer periods of time before moving on. The Supreme General learned quickly that sending his soldiers into the cedar swamp was a sure ticket to death. Another thousand Saracen soldiers died on the second day.

But that still left an army of almost fifteen thousand strong, and, at the present rate, well over ten thousand would reach the straits of Mackinaw, and that was more than enough to defeat the Shadow Militia in open combat.

On the third day, the Saracen army unexpectedly cut east over to the I 75 corridor, which was a larger highway with two lanes going south and two lanes going north. The Supreme General transported his men using all four lanes and made it all the way north of Indian River by nightfall. They were now only fifteen miles from the Mackinaw Bridge. The Supreme General sent two of the F-18s to monitor the bridge and cut off any mass escape from the lower peninsula to the Upper Peninsula. Because of this, the Shadow Militia and all four thousand soldiers were trapped at Mackinaw City.

It suddenly appeared to everyone that the Shadow Militia had been beaten and would soon make their last stand with their backs to the Straits of Mackinaw.

July 17, Shadow Militia Air Force

COLONEL MACPHERSON STOOD ON THE PAVED RUNWAY in northeastern Michigan and took stock of the Shadow Militia Air Force.

"How many aircraft in total?"

Major Fannemere was following to the left and slightly abreast of the colonel as he moved down the runway from plane to plane in their last-minute inspection.

"We have twenty-six planes and twenty-six pilots, sir."

Each pilot was standing in front of his aircraft at the position of attention. Colonel MacPherson had spent the better part of the past week traveling across the state and enlisting as many pilots as possible. It had been difficult to recruit volunteers when he had to tell them they'd be flying against F-18 fighters and Apache attack helicopters.

Colonel MacPherson stopped in front of a pilot, and stood at attention as the man looked straight ahead and rendered his best salute. Mac returned the salute with dignity and grace.

"At ease, lieutenant. What's your name?"

All the volunteers had been given temporary commissions in the Shadow Militia Air Force and had some type of gold or silver bars on their collars. This man was old, and Mac was immediately reminded of Lieutenant Harold Steffens who'd fought and died so valiantly in the Battle for Iroquois just a few months earlier.

"Lieutenant Chet Hanson, sir."

"I appreciate your willingness to fly against such heavy odds. You do realize what you'll be up against, don't you?"

The old man looked the colonel square in the eyes before replying. "Yer damn right I do."

Colonel MacPherson smiled slightly. "And you're not afraid?"

The grisly old pilot turned his head and spit off to one side. "Are you kiddin' me, Colonel? When I flew in Nam I was too young-n-dumb to be afraid. But by time my third marriage rolled around I'd learned a lot about fear." He thought a moment. "Hell yes I'm afraid! I'm skeered shitless!"

The colonel laughed softly to himself. He had to remember to tell that one to General Branch, provided they were both still alive twenty-four hours from now.

"Me too, lieutenant. Me too. But I know you'll fight with honor up there tomorrow, and there's a slight chance you might even live to brag about it."

The old lieutenant snapped to attention before responding.

"I'll take those odds, sir." Then he saluted crisply and Colonel MacPherson moved on down the runway. For just a moment he allowed himself to believe these men had a fighting chance. They had the heart; they had the attitude; they just didn't have the right planes and training.

After the full inspection, Mac sauntered off the field and into the metal-roofed Quonset hut to radio the general. For better or for worse, tomorrow they would fly – they would fly and they would die.

The Blind Man

THE BLIND MAN STARED UP AT THE SCREEN ON THE wall of his private quarters. There were problems all over the country: they'd just been attacked in the mountains of Idaho and Boise was surrounded. It would fall by this time tomorrow provided he didn't send much-needed airpower and reinforcements. In the South it was even worse. Guerilla fighters from the Smoky Mountains were coming down almost every night and wreaking havoc on his supply chain. That was fairly common, but something had changed in the last twenty-four hours. Everything had intensified as if someone had thrown a switch. And then it occurred to him. General Branch and the Shadow Militia really were in control of all the rebel forces nation-wide, and they were using these coordinated attacks to prevent him from sending reinforcements to the Saracen army in Northern Michigan.

Jared swore under his breath. He'd always wanted a worthy adversary, but … this was becoming a bit too much of a challenge. All along he'd been careful not to underestimate General Branch, but, despite that, the old man had still managed to outmaneuver him at nearly every turn. On the one hand, he didn't want to give up. He wanted to defeat Rodney T. Branch in battle. On the other hand, he wanted to survive as well.

Jared put his dark sunglasses back on and reached down to

press the intercom button. "Michael, get in here right now!"

A few seconds later a man opened the door and walked in carrying a clipboard. "Yes, sir."

Jared hated the clipboard and the little man. He didn't like things written down, and Sammy Thurmond had always been able to memorize everything. He hated pretending to be blind. In a moment of fury he threw his sun glasses down onto the desk and yelled at the man. "Get me General Holland on the line from Southern Command!"

The man just stood there in shock, not moving, not saying anything. Jared walked up to him to within ten inches of his face. He looked straight into the man's blue eyes and snarled. "Didn't you hear me? I said get General Holland on the video screen now!"

The man finally moved. "Yes, sir. Right away, sir." And then he backed toward the door, still struggling to understand what had just happened. He thought to himself *He was blind, but now he can see?* It was more than he could wrap his mind around, so he just backed out of the room as quickly as possible.

Once the other man was gone, Jared picked up his Sat phone and was soon talking to Sammy Thurmond.

"Mr. Thurmond, what is the situation there?"

As always, his assistant was brief and precise. "The Shadow Militia has retreated to Mackinaw City and by morning they will be totally surrounded. The Supreme General is attacking at dawn. The Shadow Militia is outnumbered four to one."

Jared nodded, happy that at least one area of the country was going well. "Is there any sign of the Shadow Militia Air Force?"

"No, sir."

Jared thought for a moment. There had been no sign of them in the South or in the West either. They had to be in the North. "Stay in direct contact with our air base in Ohio. Make sure the Shadow Militia's airpower is completely destroyed as soon as they enter the field of battle."

There was an uncharacteristic moment of silence, and Jared noticed it. But it was just a fleeting moment. "Yes, sir. It will be done."

And then Jared added. "And Mr. Thurmond, as soon as this is accomplished, I'd like you to return to me as quickly as possible. Keep me updated."

"Yes, sir."

The line went dead, and Sammy Thurmond stared down at the sat phone. Something was different. Did The Blind Man know about Jackie? Then he answered his own question. No, he did not. Why? Because he was still alive. But the phone call had left him more uneasy than before. He'd never sensed so much tension and uncertainty in The Blind man's voice. Something was different, and ... different was always dangerous.

The Saracen Camp Prepares

THE SUPREME GENERAL LOOKED OUT OVER THE THOUsands of camp fires in the darkness. They had finally arrived at Mackinaw City and had set up a perimeter just a mile outside the city limits. Before darkness had set in Abdul had seen the splendor of the Mackinaw Bridge. The locals called it Mighty Mac, and it was huge with its two towers rising up over five hundred feet as it separated Lake Huron from Lake Michigan. It was the third largest suspension bridge in North America, spanning five miles from shore to shore and joining Michigan's upper and lower peninsulas.

Abdul had fallen in love with the engineering marvel as soon as he'd seen it, and had vowed to make Mackinaw City the capitol of his new empire. He would live in the shadow of this giant, and it would allow him to travel to the northern half of his kingdom with ease.

His commanders had just left his quarters, and were busily preparing for the final battle in the morning. It would be an all-out attack from three sides, driving the infidels into the lake. Abdul wondered why they called it a lake. It was so huge. He would rename it the Sea of the Great Prophet, and he would drive General Branch and his army into the Straits of Mackinaw.

And then, he would turn his sights on The Blind Man.

Mackinaw Bridge, Setting the Charges

Staff Sergeant Adam Cervantes watched as his detail ran the det cord connecting each satchel of C4 together in a series. Adam had always been a bit of a pyromaniac and det cord fascinated him. Det cord was simply a high-speed fuse that exploded, rather than burned, The cord was suitable for detonating high explosives, and the velocity of detonation was sufficient to use it for synchronizing multiple charges to detonate almost simultaneously. The cord exploded at the velocity of four miles per second, and one of Adam's favorite things to do was use it to take down trees for firewood back on the farm. Of course, that had been illegal, but ... well ... he didn't live on the farm anymore, and the ATF was defunct, so ... no blood – no foul. It was military-grade explosive and he'd been assured the C4 would do the job, provided he set it up in the proper configuration. But then again, he'd never blown up the Mackinaw Bridge before, so, it was all theory to him.

He stepped out from under the southern end of the bridge and looked up at the huge suspension cables and towers. The bridge was huge, and he wasn't so sure he could do it. Despite his pyromaniacal tendencies, he felt ambivalent about blowing it up. It was so beautiful; it had been here for so many years, decades, in fact, since 1957. It would be a shame to watch it crash down into the water. But ... it was better than having to fight fifteen-thousand psychotic Saracens to the death.

Adam had been fighting alongside the Militia Rangers in the last battle, and before that he'd been helping Donny

Brewster train the new soldiers. They were a good force, as good as they could be in so short a time, but ... still ... fifteen thousand Saracens backed up by F-18s and Apaches was a big bite to swallow, and he hoped they didn't choke on it. He looked up into the sky. Sometimes he could hear the F-18s and the Apaches up there. They stayed up high, letting their radar and their thermal imaging capabilities do the surveillance job for them. If they came down low, they'd be vulnerable to Stinger missiles or other MANPAD-launched rockets, which the general seemed to have an ample supply of, but, so long as they stayed up high, their electronic countermeasures would be able to defeat the Stingers with ease. Adam knew that each of the four Hornets flying CAP above them carried one-hundred flares, rendering the Stinger missiles useless.

But, in the end, Adam knew it would all come down to General Rodney T. Branch. What did the old man have up his sleeve this time? It seemed hopeless.

But the thing that bothered Adam the most was the pilots flying CAP above them. He just didn't understand how so many American military pilots could turn traitor. It bothered him to his core. How was The Blind Man able to recruit once-patriotic Americans to slaughter fellow citizens? He would probably never know the answer to that question. He took one last look up into the star-studded summer night and then walked back underneath the bridge to continue his work of destruction.

CHAPTER 26

July 15, The Final Battle Begins

THE SUPREME GENERAL STOOD atop his Bradley fighting vehicle surveying the expanse of his army. The sun was just rising over the Lake Huron shoreline as he looked on. He knew in his heart that by sundown it would be over, and General Rodney Branch would be dead. He was about to launch the advance into town when his aid yelled up to him.

" Sir! There is urgent news from the advance scouts!"

Abdul made his way down off the Bradley and was soon standing beside the man. "What is it?"

The man looked fearful. He always hated approaching the Supreme General as people sometimes lost their heads when giving him bad news. "They have spotted twelve tanks just inside the city limits, sir. They are cleverly hidden, and could not be seen from the air."

Abdul thought for a moment before issuing orders. *Where had they come from? They weren't there last night.* It didn't matter when he had the means to destroy them. "Order the Apaches to attack. Then report back to me."

CAPTAIN VAN KRAI HAD LEFT THE AIR FORCE OF THE Netherlands shortly after The Collapse to join The Blind Man here in America. Almost all the pilots in The Blind Man's air force were non-American, but all spoke English. In the case of the Apaches flying ground support over Mackinaw City, four were from the Netherlands, three from the United Kingdom, three from Japan and two from Egypt.

Captain Van Krai was a dedicated pilot who loved the Apache, and The Blind Man was the only opportunity he'd been offered to fly, so he'd seized it as soon as it was made to him. Besides, he had no other skills, no family, and no prospects and no other realistic means of survival.

The AH-64 he flew today could support numerous roles, but today he was loaded with sixteen Hellfire missiles, whose primary mission was to attack and destroy enemy tanks and armor. He quickly confirmed receipt of target coordinates and led his six Apaches down to attack while the other six were held in reserve at a higher altitude.

"Saracen Command, this is Apache One. We are commencing our run."

They attacked in parallel, firing at all twelve tanks almost simultaneously. He was surprised to see his tank seem to vaporize when hit by the Hellfire missile. This wasn't typical hit results.

"Apache One reports direct hit. All units report in."

Captain Van Krai listened as all units reported direct hits.

"Apache Two direct hit, target destroyed."

"Apache Three direct hit, target destroyed."

"Apache Four direct hit, target destroyed."

"Apache Five direct hit, target destroyed."

"Apache Six direct hit. But … Captain. It didn't look right."

Captain Van Krai had the same nagging feeling that something wasn't right. "Apaches four, five and six go in low to assess damage. Apaches Two and Three switch to infrared imaging and circle for human threats."

The three Apache helicopters banked down and toward the town while the other three posted slightly higher to perform an overwatch function.

"Apache One, this is Apache Four. All traces of enemy armor gone. It's like they were never there."

That's when the first of six Stinger missiles were launched from hidden ground positions. Captain Van Krai watched in horror as three of his attack helicopters were struck and crashed in smoke and flames to the ground.

"Break off! Break off!"

But the warning came too late, and soon all six Apaches were gushing smoke and losing altitude.

"What the hell is going on?!"

"Evasive action!"

"More missiles incoming!"

Suddenly, the once-disciplined and professional radio commands were reduced to a barrage of frenzied chatter.

"I'm hit!"

"Bank left!"

"Damn! Damn!"

Three more of the Apaches went down in flames, as the other two picked up speed and fled the field of battle toward the south of Mackinaw City.

Down below, Supreme General Abdul Al'Kalwi looked on in horror as nine of his twelve Apaches crashed to the ground and continued to burn.

BACK IN THE CITY, HIDDEN INSIDE ONE-HUNDRED AND fifty-year-old concrete and brick buildings, all nine of the two-man Stinger teams took advantage of the confusion and packed up and hurriedly bugged out back to the waterfront. The twelve tanks they'd built the day before out of two-by-fours and thin plywood had been destroyed. Once there, they boarded the rubber rafts and floated out to the Straits of Mackinaw headed for their next attack points.

IN AN OLD LIGHTHOUSE, JUST WEST OF ST. IGNACE OFF highway US 2, General Branch and Colonel MacPherson looked to the south-east with smiles. Mac was the first to speak.

"Now that's a sight for sore eyes."

Rodney smiled. "Yep. Don't ya just love it when a plan comes together?"

Colonel MacPherson laughed out loud. "General, I just love it when you talk country and western."

Rodney looked over at him. "Well, my refined old friend, you can take the boy out of the country, but you can't take the country out of the boy."

Mac nodded. "How many more Stingers do we have here?"

Rodney watched as the smoke filtered up from across the straits. "Ebay had them a special, and we bought us a whole shit-load."

Colonel MacPherson knew the truth. The vast majority of Shadow Militia supplies had come from the US military or through foreign sources on the black market. The average citizen would be surprised to learn that every time weapons systems like the Stinger were upgraded, the older platforms had to be disposed of. With the right connections, a fair amount of money, and the proper paperwork, just about anything was possible.

Colonel MacPherson looked up high in the sky in search of the F-18s. They were mere dots above the straits, dispersed and flying a standard air patrol pattern.

"But what about the Hornets?"

Rodney took a sip of his cold coffee from the plastic, olive drab canteen he was holding. He reached up to his breast pocket for the cigarette that wasn't there.

"We have to deal with them, but … we don't have to shoot them down, at least not all of them." He was silent a moment and Mac just waited. "I have a plan."

Saracen HQ

THE SUPREME GENERAL WAS SCREAMING INTO THE SAT-phone at The Blind Man. "I need more helicopters. He shot them all down!"

The Blind Man was also furious, but he controlled his

voice. It emitted a deadly calm that caused Abdul to stop talking. "That's right, Supreme General." He spat the words out like bile. "I gave you twelve state-of-the-art attack helicopters, and you promptly crashed nine of them to the ground through your own lack of military prowess." There was a pause. "I will not waste any more of my irreplaceable military hardware on the likes of you."

Abdul was so filled with rage that he could do nothing but sputter incoherently. The Blind Man waited for him to silence before going on. "General Holland will now be taking over tactical control of the battle. He will issue commands to you through Mr. Thurmond."

There was an indecisive silence.

"But what if I kill Mr. Thurmond and proceed on my own?"

Jared laughed softly into the satphone. "Then I will send my bombers to Mackinaw City and reduce your army to blood, bones, and rubble."

A chill ran through Abdul's bones. "It, it was just … a hypothetical question." Oh, how he hated The Blind Man.

Jared Thompson disconnected the call, then made another to General Holland who then conferred with Sammy Thurmond. An hour later a full barrage of artillery, armor and mortar fire opened up on Mackinaw City. By noon the once beautiful, historic town had been reduced to smoke and rubble. Not a single stone was left upon another.

The Supreme General looked on in disgust. His new capitol city of Mackinaw was now a tomb. An hour later his entire army marched through the rubble-strewn streets in unopposed conquest. Not a single person, alive or dead, could be found. Only then did the Supreme General realize the Shadow Militia had left the night before, abandoning the town and assuring their survival to fight another day. *How had they done it without the Hornets detecting it?*

The SS Badger

"IF YOU CAN DROP US OFF NEAR WILDERNESS STATE Park near the south-western entrance to the straits, then we can move to our assigned locations in the dinghies before setting up our strike teams." Dan Branch had flown to Beaver Island in his Huey to meet up with the SS Badger before she left her anchorage for the final run through the Mackinaw Straits.

Captain John Darkfoote looked out into the early afternoon sky. It was clear now, but a bank of rain clouds was moving in from the northwest. These storms could move in fast off the Great Lakes.

"No problem. Just make sure you leave that Zodiac behind for me and the crew. When it all hits the fan I don't want to be standing in front of it. I want a fast ride out of harm's way."

Colonel Dan Branch smiled, then quickly frowned again as the Badger rolled gently on the small swells of Lake Michigan. "Roger that, Captain. I want the same thing."

The two of them had become friends in the past few days of loading and outfitting the Badger for this mission.

"You going to be okay, Dan? You look a little green around the gills."

Dan smiled weakly. "Let's just say I haven't quite got my sea legs yet."

John laughed. "No kidding. I didn't realize you were such a landlubber."

Dan rushed over to the metal trash can and heaved into it. He waited a second for the nausea to pass, then wiped his mouth with a rag he had stuffed in his waistband for just such a purpose. Captain Darkfoote laughed out loud this time, but Dan was quick to snarl back at him.

They had already moved fifteen hundred troops from Sturgeon Bay up to Brevort in the Upper Peninsula during the night. Most of them hadn't enjoyed the Great Lake's swells either and had puked for half the ride. John had found it amusing. Apparently another fifteen hundred soldiers had been moved on the Lake Huron side using the Mackinaw Island

Ferries. One thousand had remained in the lower peninsula, spread out strategically dispersed to be used during another phase of the plan. But General Branch had moved them all from Mackinaw City, thus denying the Supreme General his coveted final battle where all the odds were in his favor.

"You're really enjoying this, aren't you, Captain."

John took his hands off the wheel long enough to shrug his shoulders and lift his hands up. "Not really. Can't say I enjoy the smell of your vomit all that much."

Dan followed the edge of the bridge bulkhead over to the door. "I think I'll go out on deck and check on the last-minute preparations for departure."

The captain smiled and turned back to face the east as Dan exited the bridge. Soon he was alone again. The ship felt good beneath his feet, and he quickly realized he'd missed his calling. He spoke out loud to the emptiness. "Better late than never I suppose."

And then his thoughts turned to the attack plan that Colonel Branch had laid out for him. It was a good plan, but... he wasn't fond of the outcome, plus, it had some weaknesses. It was just too complicated with plenty of room for error. And the whole idea of just 'trusting' General Branch to take the F-18s and Apache helicopters out of the equation seemed like a large leap of faith to him.

He knew a way to eliminate the weakness, but it came with a sacrifice. And then there was the question of Eileen. How would he get her to cooperate? At any rate, he had a few more hours to think about it before making a final decision. He continued his coastwise run off the lower Peninsula shoreline on his way north to Wilderness State Park near the south-western entrance to the straits.

A half hour later ten dinghies shoved away from the Badger and headed for their predetermined strike points. On their way east from Beaver Island, they'd already dropped off ten other dinghies, each with two-man strike teams on St Helena Island. They would fan out along the southern shore of the straits as well as set up on some of the tiny islands off the coastline.

He saw Eileen making her way up to the foredeck on her way to the bridge. He'd tried to persuade her to leave with Dan, but had come up short on that one The woman was as stubborn as a mule, and, since she was incredibly young, strong and beautiful, she usually got her way.

Without warning, the pain in his chest struck again, this time with the force of a knife-edged sledgehammer. His body doubled over, and he stayed there, hoping she wouldn't see him this way. Just as the bridge door opened be straightened up with a frown on his face.

She moved toward him with concern.

"You okay, honey?"

John forced a smile. "Of course I am." And then he added. "Now that my favorite person in the world is here. Eileen blushed. She lowered her eyes and reached out for an embrace. "Thanks honey."

John hugged her back and the pain subsided.

"Honey, would you like to steer the ship? I have something I have to take care of."

Eileen's face lit up. "Sure honey!"

"Just keep steering the present heading of 350. But let me know if you see an iceberg." She raised her eyebrows at his last remark and smiled. She loved this old man and his wry and unpredictable humor.

"Icebergs. Right. I will."

John had only one preparation left to make. He gave her one last squeeze before moving from the bridge to the foredeck. He took the can of red paint and brush as he lowered himself over the bow in a bosun's chair. This was to be the crowning achievement of his life.

CHAPTER 27

The Mighty Mac

THE **SUPREME GENERAL STOOD** atop his Bradley looking out at the five-mile expanse of the Mackinaw Bridge. There were white-caps on both the Lake Michigan and Lake Huron sides of the straits and a storm was definitely coming in from the west.

He still had no idea how General Branch had moved four thousand troops to the opposite shore without using the bridge and being spotted by the F-18s on CAP above them. Once he captured the general, that was the first of many questions he would ask the man. This arrogant infidel had been tormenting him from just out of arm's reach for weeks now, striking at him from hidden positions, never coming out to fight fair, and Abdul was thirsting for General Branch's blood. In the end he would get his satisfaction and his pound of flesh.

"This end of the bridge is wired with explosives, sir. They were getting ready to blow it but the bombardment must have interrupted their work."

Abdul thought for a moment. It angered him. He already considered the magnificent bridge to be his property, part of his new kingdom, and General Branch had tried to destroy it. It also angered him that The Blind Man had been right about bombarding the town prior to attack.

"Dismantle the explosives and make it safe for us to cross the bridge. I want to be on the other side and killing kafirs before dark."

Sammy Thurmond stood about twenty feet off to the left. listening, taking it all in. He looked across the straits of Mackinaw to the Upper Peninsula. *Something didn't feel right. why hadn't General Branch blown the bridge?*

His self-preservation instincts kicked in, and he determined himself to tread carefully from here on out.

MANPADS on Parade

CAPTAIN DANNY BRIEL WAS SITTING IN THE BUSHES AT the base of the lighthouse off Round Island just south of Mackinaw Island. His rowboat with a small outboard motor was beached just a few yards away and covered with brush. He didn't know how much those F-18s could see, but he wasn't about to take any chances either.

He looked down at the metal case which housed the Stinger missile. He'd been told this was the latest Stinger configuration, and would be able to better penetrate the electronic counter-warfare flares of the F-18 Hornets. Not all the MANPAD teams had this latest version, but all were capable of taking down a Hornet, provided the jet was low and occupied on something else and not able to adequately respond to multiple threats.

In their briefing, he'd been told these Hornet pilots were from other countries, primarily Kuwait, Malaysia and Spain. That relieved Captain Briel to his core, as he had no desire to fire upon an American military pilot.

At last night's briefing, he learned all about the Hornet he was now trying to shoot down. Developed by McDonnell Douglas the F/A-18 Hornet is a twin-engine supersonic, all-weather carrier-capable multirole combat jet, designed as both a fighter and attack aircraft. It was designed primarily for use by the United States Navy and Marine Corps.

The F/A-18 has a top speed of 1,190 mph, and can carry a wide variety of bombs and missiles, including air-to-air and air-to-ground, supplemented by the 20 mm M61 Vulcan cannon. As a general rule, Danny tried to avoid being hit by missiles and cannons.

The F-18s rely on electronics countermeasures in the form of flare dispensers which, either manually or automatically shoot out flares of magnesium which burn hotter than the afterburners of a jet engine. These decoy the missile away from the jet. But Danny had the newest generation of the FIM-92 Stinger which utilized a dual infrared and ultraviolet seeker head, which allows for a redundant tracking solution, effectively negating the impact of modern decoy flares. That's what Danny had been told, and, although he didn't understand all the technical jargon, he did know how to aim and fire the Stinger missile, and that was good enough for his purposes.

Danny unpacked the Stinger and began to prepare for launch. And then ... he waited and watched.

The Bait

LIEUTENANT CHET HANSON FLEW AS CLOSE TO THE deck as he could get without crashing. His single-engine Cessna wasn't exactly state of the art, well, actually, it barely flew. Before every launch he prayed for an updraft, and at every landing he prayed for no cross winds. Chet knew he was flying today on little more than a wing and a prayer.

Engine problems had delayed him, and the other twenty-five planes had already launched so he was now struggling to catch up to the formation. His engine sputtered, forcing him to throttle back and reduce airspeed. Better not push it. He continued to fall behind the other planes, but still he pressed on.

At the final briefing they were told the truth of the situation and the unlikelihood of their survival. Despite that, all twenty-six pilots had chosen to fly into battle. Chet was old, and his wife had died over the winter, so he had little to live for. The decision had been easy for him. But he wondered about the others. So many of them were young, yet ... they were flying and fighting, knowing their young lives could be cut short.

He found himself wondering about their motives. Was it misguided glory? Was it bravery? He didn't know but expected each man flew for his own private purpose. But one thing he did know: save himself, each pilot was a hero, sacrificing himself for strangers, giving their lives so that others could live on and fight for freedom. For him, he wasn't brave. He knew that. He just wanted to end a life not worth living and be rejoined with his wife in the hereafter. There was no bravery in that. And that's when Chet realized he was a true romantic. And it made him feel good. Would his wife be proud of him, or would she scold him for his stupidity?

He shrugged in the tiny cockpit. "In a few hours, I'll be able to ask her myself."

Crossing the Rubicon

THE SUPREME GENERAL WATCHED PROUDLY AS HIS ARMY of Saracen soldiers lined up at the southern approaches to the Mighty Mac. The explosives had been removed, and several thousand of his men were already on the bridge and moving slowly to the north. The F-18 Hornet fighter-attack aircraft were high overhead. Yesterday there were only two Hornets, but today their number had increased to four. The Hornets overhead would notify them of any danger, while the remaining Apache attack helicopters stayed over Mackinaw City ready to attack any threat to the crossing army. Abdul had already prayed to Allah and his great prophet, peace be upon him, for a safe passage to the Upper Peninsula.

The joy in his heart threatened to spill out, but he determined to control himself for just a while longer. He couldn't wait to get to the other side and destroy the Shadow Militia.

A Yooper Lighthouse

"HERE THEY COME, GENERAL."
Rodney smiled as Colonel MacPherson relinquished use

of the telescope inside the lighthouse. Almost six miles off he could see the army of Saracens marching onto the bridge like lemmings. In better times he would have called in an airstrike, but …all he had right now was a force of twenty-six prop planes of dubious abilities. He had a nagging sense of guilt about his own plan. It called for too much potential sacrifice, with none of it his own. But … if the Saracen army made it to the other side, much innocent blood would be shed, and many lives would be lost.

All through his military career he'd learned the importance of keeping his battle plan simple. The more complex the plan, the more things could go wrong. But now … his options and equipment were severely limited, so he was forced to patch together forces from all over the chess board. And now … the pieces were lined up like dominoes, but if one failed to fall, the others would not follow.

Rodney had taken much of his battle plan straight from history. The harassing of the Saracen forces from mid-Michigan all the way to Mackinaw City had been the classic guerilla warfare tactic used by the colonial militias on April 19th, 1775 on the road back to Boston right after the slaughter on the green at Lexington.

Then, he'd withdrawn his forces in the night, saving them from certain destruction, similar to what General Washington had done against the British General Howe in the Battle of Long Island. It was also reminiscent of the British miracle at Dunkirk.

Most painful of all to Rodney were the planes attacking from the east. This tactic came straight from the annals of the Battle of Midway. It could potentially end in great loss of life. And he'd ordered it.

The Stinger missile attacks were derived from the Afghan freedom fighters in the war to repel the Soviet Union from Afghanistan.

But the SS Badger … that was new. And now, as all generals throughout time are forced to do, all General Branch could do was wait.

When Hornets Attack

"SARACEN HQ THIS HORNET LEADER, OVER." THE pilot spoke with a Spanish accent and then waited for confirmation.

"This is Saracen HQ, go ahead, Hornet Leader."

"Saracen HQ we have radar contact twenty-five miles due east of your location. Large formation following the nap of the earth. Approximately fifteen aircraft, moving 255 miles per hour. What are your orders?"

"This is Saracen HQ, Wait one, over."

Commander Rubio Gonzales waited impatiently overhead as the radio operator consulted with command. He'd seen the nine Apaches go down in flames just a few hours ago, and his fighter pilot instincts were on full alert but also itching for a fight. Nonetheless, he wasn't anxious to go down on the deck with short-range surface to air missiles known to be operating in the area.

"Hornet Leader, this is Saracen HQ. You are ordered to send two Hornets to engage and destroy enemy aircraft. The remaining two will stay on CAP over the straits. More planes will join you shortly, over."

"Roger that, Saracen HQ."

He thought for a moment. He enjoyed flying the Hornet, but he was not a hero. He decided to send the other flight of two Hornets to the deck, keeping his wingman close in high cover. He would wait for reinforcements before entering the fray. Commander Gonzales preferred overwhelming odds and sure victory to going down in flames by a missile fired by a mere Michigan farmer.

Blind Man HQ

JARED THOMPSON LISTENED TO THE RADIO CHATTER from the Hornets flying over the Straits of Mackinaw with delight. General Branch had finally committed his air power to the fight, and now he could utterly destroy them. It would be a severe blow to the rebel forces, and without the constant threat of retaliation by air, Jared would be free to operate more aggressively throughout the continental US.

He listened intently as General Holland ordered twelve F-16 Fighter aircraft to scramble from the airfield in Ohio to intercept and destroy the Shadow Militia Air Force. At this point he was near giddy, and had abandoned all pretense of blindness. Those around him still hadn't adapted to it, but he didn't care. The ruse of blindness had given him an edge for many years, but now, it was no longer needed. It felt good to throw off the nuisance and use his eyesight with wild abandon. Jared had wanted to send more fighters, but General Holland had advised him not to do so. There were other attacks still raging in the South where they would be needed, and the general assured him twelve F-16s along with the four Hornets would be more than a match to ambush and destroy the approaching Shadow Militia.

Jared forced himself to sit down in the recliner in front of the big screen before him. He picked up the decanter of brandy and poured a small amount. The alcohol burned all the way down. And now, all he had to do was watch and listen to the destruction of the Shadow Militia and his arch nemesis, General Rodney T. Branch.

Jared took another small sip. He so much hoped the general could be taken alive. He wanted to meet the man.

Outnumbered

"Hornet Leader we are closing on formation. We should have visual contact momentarily."

The lead F-18 and his wingman were at four thousand feet and closing. They would attack out of the setting sun from a superior altitude. They would undoubtedly fire the first shots and score overwhelming hits. The enemy formation would break apart and a dogfight would ensue. This would slow down the enemy planes long enough for the F-16s to attack from the South. Then the most unexpected thing happened.

"Hornet Leader this is Hornet Three. Radar now shows twenty-five enemy aircraft, over."

Commander Rubio Gonzales, still flying CAP high above the Straits of Mackinaw didn't respond immediately.

"Hornet Leader, this is Hornet Three. We are outnumbered twelve to one. We could use a little help down here, over."

"Hornet Leader, this is Saracen HQ. You are ordered to remain above the bridge in CAP. Hornet Three and Four proceed to attack the enemy formation, over."

Commander Gonzales looked around him and spoke on his intercom to his Weapons Systems Officer. "Keep your eyes peeled. We don't want to be caught off guard."

His WSO responded immediately. "We should go down and help them. They need us."

Rubio hesitated. He had to follow orders. Then it occurred to him. He'd been ordered to stay over the straits. No one said he couldn't circle back to the east and be closer to the fight. He slowly banked to the south and then east. His wingman stayed tight on his tail.

The SS Badger

"I WILL NOT LEAVE YOU!"

Eileen looked at him with imploring eyes. John Darkfoote was both incensed at her stubbornness and touched by her loyalty.

"You have to go now, Eileen! I don't know what's going to happen up there. I could die!"

She grabbed onto him and refused to let go. "And that's exactly why I'm not leaving this ship! If you die then I'll die right there beside you."

John Darkfoote suddenly felt ten years older, knowing that he could be responsible for her death. The others had left five minutes ago in the ship's rigid hull inflatable, and there was but one boat left, a small Zodiac.

"Eileen. I love you. You know I do. But I want you to live. This isn't some movie. It's not Romeo and Juliet, all filled with romance and excitement." He pointed up into the sky. "Those are F-18 fighter jets up there, and they're going to try and sink this boat. I have to make sure it gets to the bridge before that happens."

She grabbed his face in her hands. "So you admit it! You're going to die!"

John rolled his eyes up toward the bridge and tried to push her away as he spoke. "No, no! You stubborn woman! I'm going to put it on autopilot as soon as we get close enough, and then I'll jump overboard and swim back to shore. I'm a very good swimmer."

"But what about the fighter jets?"

John grabbed her by the shoulders and turned her to face him. "The general has promised to take them out. I'll be safe. I promise you."

Up ahead John could see the twin towers of the Mackinaw Bridge looming up into the sky. In a few minutes they'd be there, and it would be too late for her.

"Listen sweetheart, I'm an old man and you're young. You need to live a long time yet and have babies and raise a family."

Eileen started to cry, but he didn't stop talking. "Look at me, honey. I'm sick. Very sick. I haven't told you this, but I think I'm dying. Even if I survive I won't be alive for long."

She stopped crying and looked up at him. "Weren't you going to tell me?"

John threw up his hands in despair, suddenly understanding why he'd never married. This woman just would not give up.

"You were dying and you weren't going to share it with me! I thought we didn't have any secrets from each other!"

John grabbed his face with both hands and shook from side

to side. "Oh, for the love of God!"

And that's when he heard the engines of the three Apache attack helicopters. Eileen heard them too, and they both looked out to the starboard bow and saw black shapes above the horizon between them and the bridge. Steadily they came closer. John looked back at her one last time. "Last chance, kid. Please leave the ship."

Her response was to shake her head from side to side and then kiss him full on the lips. "What can I do to help?"

Stinger Alley

HORNET THREE LOOKED DOWN AT HIS RADAR SCREEN and watched the large group of green blips as they moved closer and closer. There was more than a little fear in his guts as his imagination wondered what kind of aircraft they were up against. He thought to himself, *how bad could it be?* He'd been told they were likely to be inferior to his Hornet.

That's when the blips disappeared. One by one they simply dropped off his screen and were gone from all reality. The voice of his WSO spoke his next thoughts verbatim. "What the hell?" Hornet Three waited a few seconds longer before reporting in.

"Hornet Leader, this is Hornet Three. The enemy planes appear to be gone now." He leveled out and continued to cruise past an island with a lighthouse a few thousand feet below.

"Hornet Three, this is Hornet Leader, say again your last, over."

"Hornet Leader, I can say it a hundred times more if you like, but that won't change the reality. Those planes are gone. Our radar shows no enemy planes, sir."

THE BLIND MAN COULD SCARCELY BELIEVE HIS EARS. HE lowered the brandy from his lips without taking a drink. He was alone in the room, but he spoke aloud "What the …"

And then it got worse.

DANNY BRIEL WAITED UNTIL THE F-18 PASSED HIS LOCA-
tion at the lighthouse before firing the Stinger. The five-foot
long missile was pushed out of the launcher by a small ejec-
tion motor to a safe distance before engaging the two-stage
solid-fuel sustainer. The missile accelerated to the speed of
Mach 2 as it headed for the tail of the Hornet. He watched the
trail of smoke as it streaked away from him. Then it occurred
to him, *I should get the hell outta here.*

"HORNET LEADER, THIS IS HORNET THREE. I'VE JUST
lost my wingman! I say again. My wingman is down."

That's when he heard his Weapons Systems Officer scream
into his ear. "We've got multiple missiles headed our way.
Releasing countermeasures now!"

Hornet Three moved to full throttle and began its near-
vertical climb off the deck. The first three Stinger missiles
followed the countermeasure flares, but the next one was not
fooled. It streaked up and flew to within just a few yards of the
huge exhaust nozzles of the Hornet before detonating.

"Hornet Three, this is Hornet Leader, over."

There was no answer.

"Hornet Three, this is Hornet Leader, over."

Rubio's heart sank in his chest when he realized he should
have come sooner. By now they were well east of the straits
and outside their patrol zone.

"Hornet Two, stay on my six and follow me up. Let's get
away from those missiles."

They began to climb, which took them even further
from the Mackinaw Bridge. His radio crackled to life, and
Commander Gonzales listened to HQ while the feeling of
dread filled him to his core.

"Hornet Leader, this is Saracen HQ, over."

He waited a few seconds before responding, focusing
on his climb away from danger. "Saracen HQ this is Hornet
Leader, go ahead, over."

"Hornet Leader, we have a large boat approaching from due west of the bridge. You are to attack and sink."

Rubio let the words hover in his mind for a moment. A large boat? How large? He didn't have any armaments on board that were designed to take out a ship! During the briefing they'd told everyone to be prepared for air-to-air combat, and that's how the Hornets had been armed, strictly with guns and air-to-air missiles. If only he had a Harpoon, but ... he didn't. But Rubio acknowledged. "Saracen HQ, this is Hornet Leader. Roger that we will comply." Upon reaching altitude, he leveled out and banked to the west, knowing full well he might not make it in time.

SS Badger, 2 Miles from Mighty Mac

THE FIRST ROCKET HIT THEM JUST AFT OF THE BRIDGE, opening up bulkheads and overheads all around. John and Eileen were knocked to the deck. Eileen didn't get back up, but John forced himself to crawl over to her. The second rocket hit below them and he felt both their bodies being lifted off the deck before slamming back down. John heard an explosion and then another and another as he waited for the next rocket to kill them both. The overhead of the wheelhouse was ripped open by the collapsing foremast stack, letting a ten-mile-an-hour wind push in and blow on his back. The air brought him around and he groggily pulled himself up to his feet just in time to see all three Apache helicopters plummeting to the water in smoke and flames. He could still see the contrails of the Stinger missiles fading from view.

The wind was in his face now, and it seemed to bring him back to his senses. There was a piece of jagged wood sticking out of his left arm with blood flowing freely. Eileen still wasn't moving. He went to her rolled her over and saw the shrapnel lodged in her right temple. Her dead eyes stared up at him like a ghost. Anger surged through his body as he pushed himself back to his feet and moved to the damaged bulkhead.

He saw the binoculars still hanging beside the wheel by the leather strap and picked them up. He focused on the bridge and saw thousands of soldiers with tanks and trucks and Bradley Fighting Vehicles across the entire span. Some of them had already reached the Upper Peninsula and were pouring out into the paved parking lot beside the toll booths.

Eileen was dead. They'd killed her! Only then did he realize how much he loved her. Fueled by rage, he moved to the wheel and made a slight correction. He tried to engage the autopilot, but it no longer worked. The old engines were fine, and he was still making eighteen miles per hour. He would be there in just a few short minutes. He looked down onto the deck and saw the Satellite Phone he'd been given to use as a detonator. It was still intact. He looked down at Eileen's body. All he had to do was make the call. All his pain would end, and the people who did this …

He quickly retrieved the satphone. He only had about thirty more seconds.

THE BLIND MAN STOOD TO HIS FEET AS HIS APACHES exploded and crashed to the water below. Two of his Hornets were gone along with all his Apaches in the region. It was a devastating loss. He took another drink, this time guzzling directly from the crystal decanter. But he could still salvage it all if the Saracens made it to the other side. And then he wondered out loud. "What is on that damn ship?"

TEN MILES EAST OF THE BRIDGE, LIEUTENANT CHET Hanson looked down and saw twenty-some planes ditched in the waters of Lake Huron. Some of them had already sunk out of sight, but the pilots were bobbing up and down in orange life preservers. Chet breathed a sigh of relief, knowing that at least this part of the attack had gone as planned. He pondered whether to turn back or to ditch himself with the others. He looked to the west and saw small pillars of smoke rising from just west of the bridge's twin towers. A rush of adrenaline surged through him and he decided to check it out.

THE SUPREME GENERAL HALTED HIS BRADLEY IN THE middle of the Mackinaw Bridge and gazed at the SS Badger as it continued toward him. The topside decks were blown off, and smoke rose from a few fires from the passenger lounges and crew deck and storerooms as the boilers continued to churn energy. Abdul got a bad feeling in the pit of his stomach, and then the eerie sound of music came to him from the direction of the ghostly ship. He looked down at the bow where the name "SS Badger" had been crossed out and replaced with "Edmund Fitzgerald." The black clouds coming in from the west were over them now, as slashing sheets of rain cascaded down.

CAPTAIN JOHN DARKFOOTE HAD WRAPPED A RAG around his arm to stem the bleeding, but he was already weak from loss of blood. He was still at the wheel and they were almost upon Mighty Mac. People were shooting at him now, but he no longer cared. He was determined to die. He looked down at Eileen's body and softly said, "This one's for you, kid."

And then he pressed a button on the CD Player. The eerie music rang out and upward toward the bridge through the speakers on the SS Badger. The dark clouds enveloped the ghostly ship as it plowed through the storm.

The voice of Gordon Lightfoot could be heard clearly by every Saracen as they stared out through the storm at the spectre moving toward them.

"The legend lives on from the Chippewa on down
of the big lake they called "Gitche Gumee."
The lake, it is said, never gives up her dead
when the skies of November turn gloomy."

EVEN SUPREME GENERAL ABDUL AL'KALWI, DEVOTED Muslim, raised in the Middle East, even Abdul knew about this song. And he knew the Edmund Fitzgerald was a ship of death.

"Sink that boat! Sink it! Sink it now! Get off the bridge!"

The sound of terror in their fearless leader's voice caused a panic, and hundreds of soldiers began to run toward both ends of the bridge back toward shore. People were trampled in the confusion, slipped off the bridge in the rain and plunged to the waves below.

"Sink that boat!" Finally, one soldier manned the 7.62 mm machine gun and swung it around to open fire on the ship.

CHET HANSON SAW WHAT WAS LEFT OF THE BADGER just pulling up to the center of the bridge. He saw the machine gun on the Bradley open up and struggle to put bullets on target. Plumes of water shot up in front of its bow.

Then he saw the most heartbreaking and inspiring sight of his life. A man was standing at the helm of the ship, holding onto the wheel as bullets flew all around him. It was only a matter of time before he would be killed and the plan would end in failure.

Without thinking, Lieutenant Hanson kicked the rudder hard to the left and then banked down out of the sky straight toward the center of the bridge.

THE SUPREME GENERAL HEARD THE SCREAM OF THE Cessna as it plummeted toward him. He quickly ascertained the danger to himself and pointed up into the rain. "Shoot that plane! Shoot the plane!" Then he looked down at the Badger again and yelled "Shoot that boat!"

All the while Gordon Lightfoot kept singing through the storm.

Lake Huron rolls, Superior sings
in the rooms of her ice-water mansion.

"Shoot that boat!"

Old Michigan steams like a young man's dreams;
the islands and bays are for sportsmen.

"Shoot the plane!"

And farther below Lake Ontario
takes in what Lake Erie can send her,

Chet Hanson gritted his teeth as the machine gun swung up to meet him and the bullets tore into the cockpit. He smiled and then crashed into the Bradley Fighting vehicle.

Captain John Darkfoote held the satphone in his hand. He looked down at Eileen, punched in a few numbers.

The legend lives on from the Chippewa on down
of the big lake they call "Gitche Gumee."

John's thumb hovered over the 'send' button And then he heard the mighty scream of two F-18 Hornet attack jets as they came down low on the water behind him.

Hornet Three and Hornet Four fired all their ordinance in a last-ditch effort to stop the boat. John's thumb came down on the satphone's 'send' button.

"Superior," they said, "never gives up her dead
when the gales of November come early!"

The Sidewinder missiles hit the boilers, causing an explosion below decks which quickly spread to the cargo deck. The first thing to ignite was a propane tank truck.

The Badger disintegrated as the entire load of nitromethane, diesel fuel and Ammonium Nitrate combusted. The center of the Mighty Mac ceased to exist. Five thousand men were immediately turned to jelly and thrown into the big lakes. With the center of the bridge gone, each of the twin towers fell, one to the north and the other to the south. They collapsed onto the remaining Saracens, killing them outright or drowning them in the deep waters.

CAPTAIN DANNY BRIEL THROTTLED BACK THE MOTOR

on his small boat when he saw the Mighty Mac fall into the deep. He saw the large wave coming toward him and struggled to turn the little boat around and head back to the lighthouse. He didn't make it. His boat was lifted up and hurled onto the beach as water broke over him. He clung to the trunk of a small tree as the water subsided back into the straits. After several seconds of choking, he sucked air into his lungs. Danny sat up and looked out into the straits. Mighty Mac had fallen. But so had the Saracen Army. The straits were once again empty as they had been since the dawn of creation. Danny lay back down on the wet sand and stared straight up into the rain. And then, just as quickly as it had started, the storm subsided, the sun came out, and a flock of sea gulls landed down on the beach beside him. Profound as ever, Danny's only words were, "Holy shit-n-shinola!"

ON THE SOUTHERN SHORE, HIGH ATOP AN OLD CHURCH bell tower, Sammy Thurmond looked on and smiled in awe and respect.

CHAPTER 28

The Clean Up

IT TOOK THE BETTER OF TWO WEEKS TO hunt down the remaining Saracens. Those who resisted were killed. Those who surrendered were sent back to Detroit. When it was all over, everyone returned to their homes.

Jackie, Dan, Jeremy and baby Donna travelled back to Iroquois along with the other Militia Rangers. Sheriff Leif returned to his wife and child and set to work picking up the tattered pieces of war.

Sergeant Donny Brewster had dinner with Lisa Vanderbogh and continued his attempt to win her heart. He was successful … eventually.

In a special ceremony, the second in just a few months' time, the dead were honored at the church in Iroquois City. Captain John Darkfoote was memorialized and a granite monument was erected in his honor. Lieutenant Chet Hanson received a posthumous medal for his bravery and sacrifice. The names were read and the bugles sounded.

The Courthouse

"WHAT IS THE BLIND MAN GOING TO DO NOW, UNCLE Rodney?"

His uncle didn't say anything at first. He just picked up his coffee cup and took a sip. Dan waited patiently beside Sheriff Leif. He took the moment to sip his coffee as well.

"War is a series of moves and counter moves."

He took the six-inch length of white PVC pipe out of the cargo pocket of his pants and rolled it back and forth in his palms. He still hadn't opened it. For all he knew it was a bomb, or a tracking device, but ... he didn't think so. He would give it to Agent Jeff Arnett for analysis and scanning.

He looked up at Dan and Joe and smiled.

"It's his move. Now we wait."

EPILOGUE

THE BLIND MAN SAT IN HIS RECLINER, sipping twelve-year-old scotch. His anger had subsided, but he wouldn't be entirely rational for some time. Calmly, he picked up his satphone. and punched a few buttons.

"General Holland. I have a mission for you of extreme importance." He paused. "I would like you to deliver a message to one General Rodney T. Branch." He took a sip of his scotch. "Yes, that's right. Make it one of our bigger tactical nukes. Make it your top priority. I want it done by tomorrow, and I want it videotaped for my collection. Better yet, I'd like to watch it in real time."

He placed the phone back down on the South American coffee table and leaned back in his chair to relax.

Then he said out loud to himself.

"Okay, General Branch. You have my undivided attention now."

Coming soon!

The saga continues in

—*The Blind Man's Rage*—

Books by Skip Coryell

We Hold These Truths
Bond of Unseen Blood
Church and State
Blood in the Streets
Laughter and Tears
RKBA: Defending the Right to Keep and Bear Arms
Stalking Natalie
The God Virus
The Shadow Militia
The Saracen Tide

Skip Coryell lives with his wife and children in Michigan. He works full time as a professional writer, and "*The Saracen Tide*" is his tenth published book. He is an avid hunter and sportsman, a Marine Corps veteran, and a graduate of Cornerstone University. You can listen to Skip as he co-hosts the syndicated military talk radio show Frontlines of Freedom on www.frontlinesof-freedom.com.

For more details on Skip Coryell, or to contact him personally, go to his website at www.skipcoryell.com

Made in the USA
Charleston, SC
20 April 2015